Highlander Pledged

Stolen Highland Hearts

JAYNE CASTEL

WINTER MIST PRESS

All characters and situations in this publication are fictitious, and any resemblance to living persons is purely coincidental.

Highlander Pledged, by Jayne Castel

Copyright © 2021 by Jayne Castel. All rights reserved. No part of this publication may be reproduced, stored in a retrieval system, or transmitted in any form or by any means—electronic, mechanical, recording, or otherwise—without the prior written permission of the author.

Published by Winter Mist Press

Edited by Tim Burton
Cover design by Winter Mist Press
Cover photography courtesy of www.shutterstock.com
Dagger vector image courtesy of www.pixabay.com

Visit Jayne's website: www.jaynecastel.com

***

To my wonderful readers—thank you for coming along with me on this adventure!

***

Historical Romances by Jayne Castel

DARK AGES BRITAIN

The Kingdom of the East Angles series
Dark Under the Cover of Night (Book One)
Nightfall till Daybreak (Book Two)
The Deepening Night (Book Three)
The Kingdom of the East Angles: The Complete Series

The Kingdom of Mercia series
The Breaking Dawn (Book One)
Darkest before Dawn (Book Two)
Dawn of Wolves (Book Three)
The Kingdom of Mercia: The Complete Series

The Kingdom of Northumbria series
The Whispering Wind (Book One)
Wind Song (Book Two)
Lord of the North Wind (Book Three)
The Kingdom of Northumbria: The Complete Series

DARK AGES SCOTLAND

The Warrior Brothers of Skye series
Blood Feud (Book One)
Barbarian Slave (Book Two)
Battle Eagle (Book Three)
The Warrior Brothers of Skye: The Complete Series

The Pict Wars series
Warrior's Heart (Book One)
Warrior's Secret (Book Two)
Warrior's Wrath (Book Three)
The Pict Wars: The Complete Series

Novellas
Winter's Promise

MEDIEVAL SCOTLAND

The Brides of Skye series
The Beast's Bride (Book One)
The Outlaw's Bride (Book Two)
The Rogue's Bride (Book Three)
The Brides of Skye: The Complete Series

The Sisters of Kilbride series
Unforgotten (Book One)
Awoken (Book Two)
Fallen (Book Three)
Claimed (Epilogue novella)

The Immortal Highland Centurions series
Maximus (Book One)
Cassian (Book Two)
Draco (Book Three)
The Laird's Return (Epilogue festive novella)

Stolen Highland Hearts series
Highlander Deceived (Book One)
Highlander Entangled (Book Two)
Highlander Forbidden (Book Three)
Highlander Pledged (Book Four)

Guardians of Alba series
Nessa's Seduction (Book One)
Fyfa's Sacrifice (Book Two)
Breanna's Surrender (Book Three)

Epic Fantasy Romances by Jayne Castel

Light and Darkness series
Ruled by Shadows (Book One)
The Lost Swallow (Book Two)
Path of the Dark (Book Three)
Light and Darkness: The Complete Series

Love all, trust a few, do wrong to none.
—William Shakespeare

1
WINTER'S CHILL

Castle Gunn
Caithness, Scotland

Winter, 1429

ROBINA OLIPHANT REINED in her horse, her gaze settling upon her destination.

Castle Gunn.

The last place in Scotland she wanted to be—and yet she'd shortly be swallowed within its stone maw.

The castle perched upon an exposed finger of land and looked as if it would topple into the sea at any moment. It appeared even grimmer than usual today, its grey stone walls dark against a stormy sky as the gloaming settled over them.

Within the shadow of her fur-lined hood, Robina grimaced.

Lord, this was an awful, bleak place. Over the years, her father had dragged her on several trips south to Castle Gunn in the hope of finding a husband for her—and this time, he would actually succeed.

A biting wind howled around the fortress, bringing with it stinging needles of ice.

Robina's shoulders rounded. Despite her thick cloak, winter's chill drilled into the marrow of her bones. She could no longer feel her feet, and her gloved fingers, which clutched the reins, were frozen into claws.

She needed to get indoors, needed to wrap her hands around a steaming cup of mulled wine near a roaring fire.

But such was her dislike of this castle, and the men who resided within it, that she'd have preferred to stay outdoors, even when cold blanketed the world.

"Hurry yerself up, lass!" Her father's hearty voice cut through the wind and intruded upon Robina's brooding. Up ahead, Ramsay Oliphant turned in the saddle and gestured to his daughter. "This isn't the weather to be tarrying in!"

"Aye." Her mother's irritated voice responded. Robina glanced left to see Isla Oliphant draw her horse up alongside her. "I swear, if I have to ride much longer, I shall perish!"

Her mother's already ruddy cheeks and long, thin nose were even redder than usual, chapped by the wind and cold. Her mouth was drawn up with discomfort.

Robina imagined her own face looked just as miserable—although for different reasons to her mother's.

Clenching her jaw, Robina urged her mount on, following her father across the headland toward the rickety bridge that spanned the gap between the cliffs and the rock on which Castle Gunn perched.

Her horse, a sturdy cob of a usually unflappable temperament, snorted nervously as the Oliphant party clattered across the bridge toward the gates.

Robina made the mistake of looking down then, her gaze resting upon the sharp rocks and foaming surf below. Her head spun, dizziness catching at her throat.

Judas, how she hated heights.

Swallowing hard, she tore her attention away from the perilous drop to the razor-like teeth of the raised portcullis before her.

Dread coiled in her belly—*into the jaws of the beast.*

The three of them clattered into Castle Gunn's wide bailey, followed shortly after by the four warriors of their escort. A large covered wagon brought up the rear.

Sliding down from her horse, Robina turned an anxious eye to where the hide sides of the wagon billowed and snapped with the wind. "Please take the goshawks to the mews," she called to the wagon driver.

"He can bring in our trunks first," Isla Oliphant piped up, irritation making her tone snappish.

"My hawks can't stay out here, Ma," Robina replied. She didn't argue with her parents on most things—not these days anyway—but her goshawks were her joy and solace. She imagined Moth and Thistle hunched on their perches, seething under their leather hoods. They needed to be homed as soon as possible in the mews and fed some fresh meat for their supper.

Her mother made an impatient clucking noise before motioning to their escort. "The men will take care of everything, *including* yer hawks." Lady Oliphant had a habit of speaking as loftily as if she were the Queen of Scotland rather than a clan-chief's wife. Isla then caught her daughter by the arm and steered her, none too gently, toward the keep. "Come, let's get inside where it's warm."

Despite Robina's reluctance to set foot inside, Castle Gunn's great hall was a welcoming sight after the chill outdoors. A huge hearth roared at either end of the rectangular space, and although the air smelled of burning peat, damp wool, and wet dog, a sigh of relief gusted out of Robina.

Thankfully, the great hall was virtually empty at this time, for supper was still an hour away. Only one or two servants moved about, scrubbing down the long trestle tables and setting out wooden plates and eating knives for the coming meal.

Grateful for the reprieve—for she would see the hated Gunns soon enough—Robina headed straight for the nearest fire. An old Highland Collie was curled up before it—a shaggy grey and white bitch, who rose to her feet and wagged her tail tiredly at Robina's approach.

Despite her weariness and low mood, Robina's mouth lifted at the edges. The dog nuzzled her hand, and she fondled its fluffy ears.

"Don't touch that creature, dear ... it'll give ye fleas."

Robina ignored her mother's words and the woman herself as Lady Oliphant pushed in next to her daughter, extending her fingers, swollen from cold, before the fire.

Instead, Robina smiled down at the collie's soulful brown eyes. Ever since she'd been wee, she'd loved animals—and had found solace in their companionship. Unlike people, they didn't try to change or control her.

"I know yer father is keen to see ye wed to Tavish Gunn as soon as possible," Isla went on. "But making us travel in such cold weather is barbaric."

Robina nodded absently, hardly taking her mother's comment in, before casting a look over her shoulder at the door. She'd expected her father to follow them in here, yet he'd remained outdoors to oversee his men. Indeed, her heart had sunk when he'd announced over bannocks one morning the week previous that, now the Gunns had a new clan-chief, Tavish Gunn was ready to take a wife—and wished that wife to be Robina Oliphant.

"All the same, I thought that yer chance to catch yerself a Gunn had gone." Her mother sniffed. "After Alexander Gunn disappointed us all."

Robina's mouth thinned. That hadn't been a disappointment to *her*. When George Gunn's firstborn had fallen out with his father and been disowned, she'd been giddy with relief.

Alexander Gunn—a huge brute with wild dark hair, storm-grey eyes, and a silver scar slashing down his left cheek—had terrified her.

She'd told her father she didn't want to wed the man, yet Ramsay Oliphant had dismissed her desires. "Ye shall wed whom I say, lass," he'd roared, slamming his fist down upon the table in an uncharacteristic display of temper. "The Oliphants and the Gunns *will* be united in marriage. I won't be thwarted!"

"I can't believe Alexander Gunn took up with that Mackay woman," Isla continued with a scowl. "Aye, she is a chieftain's daughter, yet *ye* are the daughter of a clan-chief!"

Robina didn't answer. Instead, she stroked the collie's neck as it leaned into her.

Even two years on, whispers still traveled the Highlands about how the fierce Alexander Gunn had forfeited his birthright and thrown everything away to be with Jaimee Mackay. Robina had heard that the pair were now wed and had a bairn. Gunn had been accepted by the Mackays and worked as a blacksmith at Farr Castle.

Robina had been stunned by the news. Alexander Gunn hadn't been the man she'd imagined—on those few occasions they'd met, she'd thought him to be as ruthless and ambitious as his father. But he'd given it all up—and now that George Gunn was dead, the second son had stepped into the role of clan-chief.

Tavish Gunn: the man she was to wed.

And as if thinking about the devil summoned him, the doors to the great hall opened and a tall leather-clad figure with a fur-lined cloak rippling from his shoulders stalked in.

Robina went rigid, her gaze tracking his path toward her.

Although the new Gunn clan-chief lacked his older brother's formidable musculature and size, he still managed to dominate the room.

Tavish Gunn's gaze—the grey of storm clouds—met hers, and his step faltered. An instant later, he halted.

Robina wasn't one to hold a man's eye. Her mother had instructed her years earlier that men found it challenging and irksome, and so—the biddable daughter that she was—Robina had taken her advice to heart. She'd rarely met Alexander Gunn's gaze either, for the man had scared her witless after all, yet his brother didn't provoke the same terrified response.

She barely remembered Tavish from her earlier trips to Castle Gunn—she'd been too focused on making herself invisible—and so she studied him now. He had a handsome, if slightly hawkish, face and long black hair that was presently tangled by wind and rain.

The moments drew out, and Robina realized she had looked at him too long. Swallowing hard, she dipped her head just as her mother turned from the hearth.

"Laird Gunn," Isla greeted him with a simpering tone that made Robina clench her jaw. Her mother had two faces. The first she wore before men—it was meek, sweet, and obliging. But her second mask she wore before women—and that one was bossy, prattling, and opinionated.

Robina had never seen Isla Oliphant contradict her husband.

Never.

"Lady Oliphant," Tavish Gunn acknowledged Isla coolly. Robina glanced up to see his gaze was still trained upon *her*. He wore a penetrating expression that made Robina's skin prickle. "Ye are late."

"Aye," Isla simpered. "I do apologize for our tardiness … the weather turned against us, I'm afraid."

"I was about to ride out myself to see if any harm had befallen ye," he replied, his attention never leaving Robina's face.

She had the impression he was speaking directly to her, even if Isla was the one conversing with him.

"How gallant of ye," Robina's mother said before a sigh gusted out of her. "I must admit, the journey was wearisome."

Tavish Gunn nodded before moving closer to the hearth. His attention dipped to where the Highland Collie still pressed against Robina's damp skirts. The corners of his mouth then lifted.

"I see ye have met Misty."

"Aye," Isla sniffed, a groove forming between her eyebrows. "I must say, the hound reeks."

Robina cut her mother an irritated glance. "No, she doesn't." They were the first words she'd spoken since Gunn's entrance and so quietly uttered that she wondered if the clan-chief had even heard her.

"Misty is an old lass," he murmured. He paused then, a cheek dimpling as he smiled. "For years, she kept our castle's livestock safe from predators, and she's now earned her place by the fire."

As if realizing she was the subject of conversation, the shaggy collie's tail started to thump on the wooden floor.

"It's a pleasure to see ye again, Robina," Gunn said after a pause. "I have been looking forward to this day for a while now."

Isla made a clucking sound of approval, her cheeks flushing as she drew herself up with pride. Heat also flushed Robina's cheeks, although the reason for it was mortification rather than pleasure.

Dropping her gaze to her muddied boots, Robina checked the urge to pick up her skirts and flee from the hall.

Tavish Gunn had been looking forward to this?

She barely remembered the man, yet from the gleam she'd spied in his eyes, he couldn't wait to make her his bride.

2

THIS TIME TOMORROW

SHE HADN'T RESPONDED in the way he hoped.

As Tavish had stepped into the great hall, he'd imagined a demure smile, a gentle greeting.

Yet he'd received neither.

Old Misty had glued herself to Robina Oliphant's leg, reveling in the attention the young woman was giving her—yet his bride-to-be hadn't even raised a smile for him.

She was staring resolutely at the floor now as if studying the grain of the worn oak. Her pretty face and elfin features were taut.

As if sensing her daughter's diffidence, Lady Oliphant stepped forward. Mother and daughter didn't look much alike, Tavish noted. Robina was small and fey with delicate beauty, while her mother was much taller and rake-thin. The woman had a high-colored face, sharp blue eyes, and a long red-tipped nose.

"And of course, Robina has also been looking forward to seeing *ye* again, laird," the irritating woman gushed. "I apologize for her silence ... she is merely shy and weary after our journey."

"That is to be expected," Tavish rumbled, his gaze shifting back to Robina. The lass looked as if she was going to bolt at any moment.

"I understand that the wedding will take place on the morrow, as planned?" Lady Oliphant continued.

Tavish nodded. "If yer daughter is happy with that date?" he replied, his irritation rising.

"Of course she is," Lady Oliphant said with an emphatic nod.

"I'd prefer to assure myself directly from yer daughter, Lady Oliphant," Tavish answered, his tone cooling. The Lord preserve him from this interfering woman.

Lady Oliphant cut her daughter a beseeching look. However, when Robina didn't reply, she moved close to her and dug a bony elbow into her ribs.

Robina tensed, her chin jerking upward. She then, albeit reluctantly, met his eye. "Aye," she murmured, with as much enthusiasm as if he'd invited her to take part in a bloody battle the following day. "I am ready."

Ready. That wasn't the same as 'happy'. Tavish had expected a warmer welcome.

He'd 'hoped' for a warmer welcome.

He'd wanted Robina for years now—ever since her first visit to Castle Gunn four years earlier. She'd barely been of marriageable age then, yet her father had been eager to find her a match—and there were few as good as a Gunn heir.

But after his first-born's disgrace, George Gunn had ceased his invitations to Ramsay Oliphant. Tavish had been bitter about that, yet every time he brought up the subject, had suggested *he* could wed Robina, his father had snarled at him. George Gunn didn't like to be reminded of Alex's disgrace, of how he'd given up everything for Jaimee Mackay.

But now George Gunn was dead—taken by a massive seizure one afternoon—and the old man was barely in the ground before Tavish issued an offer of marriage to Robina Oliphant. He'd waited long enough.

Realizing he wasn't likely to get much out of Robina at present, Tavish took a step back and nodded. "Then tomorrow it is," he said briskly. "I shall let ye both retire to yer chambers now ... the servants have readied them on the top floor of the keep." He shifted his attention back to Robina then, wishing she'd raise those limpid hazel eyes once again. "I shall see ye both at supper."

Robina Oliphant wasn't any more garrulous at supper than she had been earlier.

However, it didn't help that her father never ceased his prattle. The man seemed to abhor silence.

"And so," Ramsay Oliphant went on, helping himself to a slice of roast pork. "I was hoping to lease some of yer land next spring ... The Ida Valley would be ideal."

"And what would ye be using it for?" Evan, one of Tavish's four younger brothers asked with a scowl. "That's good land."

"Aye," Oliphant agreed with an eager nod of his head. "I am buying in a new mob of Shetland sheep and need grazing for them." He paused then, perhaps noting the frowns on the faces of the Gunns surrounding him. "Of course ... I'd share the profits with ye," he added.

Tavish raised a pewter goblet of bramble wine to his lips. "Aye, that goes without saying, Ramsay," he replied. Annoyance simmered within him; he and Robina weren't even wed yet, and the man was making demands. "But we'll speak of this closer to spring, shall we?"

Ramsay Oliphant's full mouth pursed. He was a heavy-featured man with his greying hair pulled back at the nape. "If I'm going to put in an order for the Shetlands, I'll need to do so before—"

"We'll speak of this later," Tavish cut in, his voice a drawl. Cods, this man was a boor. It was a testament to how much Tavish wanted his daughter that he put up with him.

Tavish shifted his gaze to Robina, his attention lingering upon her. She was even lovelier than he remembered. Seated between her parents, she wore a dark-green kirtle made of heavy wool. The garment was low-cut, revealing the gentle swell of her pale breasts. She'd matured since he'd seen her last—was now much more woman than lass. In the past, she'd worn her light brown hair braided and coiled around the crown of her head—a severe style. But tonight it was unbound, falling in soft waves over her slender shoulders.

Robina ate her supper in small, neat bites, her gaze rarely straying from the platter before her.

Frustration rippled through Tavish. He wanted her to glance up and meet his eye again, yet she refused.

Tavish clenched his jaw. Alex hadn't wanted Robina. "She's too meek for me," he'd once informed Tavish. "I don't want a mouse for a wife."

Tavish had rejoiced at his brother's lack of interest in the lass *he'd* developed an obsession with. Even so, he'd disagreed with him. Robina Oliphant wasn't a meek mouse—she was reserved and shy—both traits he found appealing.

She'll warm to me once we've wed, he told himself, taking another sip of wine. *Once we get to know each other.*

"Lady Robina," he addressed her directly then. "My men tell me ye have brought two goshawks with ye. Are ye a keen hawker then?"

That got her attention. Robina's chin kicked up, her gaze widening. Her lips parted then as she readied herself to answer.

"It isn't a particularly feminine interest, I'll admit," Ramsay Oliphant cut in, his grizzled brows knitting together, "but the lass can be willful on some things."

Tavish fought the smile that tugged at his mouth. *Willful.*

Robina's high cheekbones blushed at that, and she swallowed.

"It wasn't a criticism," Tavish drawled, snaring Robina's gaze with his. Finally, she'd looked up from her supper. "I too enjoy hawking," he murmured. "What are yer hawks' names?"

Robina stared back at him, her blush deepening. "Moth and Thistle," she eventually replied. The low, husky timbre of her voice made Tavish's belly tighten, desire arrowing through his groin. How many times over the past years had he fantasized about that voice, huskier still as she gasped his name in the throes of passion?

If he was honest, Robina Oliphant had become something of a fixation of late. He'd once sneered at Alex's infatuation with Jaimee Mackay, but he no longer viewed it with disdain.

A woman could cast a spell over a man—consume him. When his father had denied him Robina, after Alexander's departure, it had been the only time in his life that Tavish had considered rising up against the old man.

Instead, he'd choked down his anger and waited—and just as well, for George Gunn was now dead, and this time tomorrow, Robina Oliphant would be his wife.

"They are bonny names," Tavish replied with a smile. "I look forward to seeing yer hawks hunt."

"Fill yer horn up, Tav!" Roy slurred drunkenly, lurching across the table with a jug of mead. "Enjoy yer last night of freedom."

Mead sloshed over the rim of the jug, soaking the sleeve of Tavish's lèine.

Irritated, he jerked the half-full horn of mead he was still struggling through out of his brother's reach, causing more mead to spill across the table. "No more ... I'm done."

"Done?" Roy sneered. "Satan's bollocks, ye drink like a lass."

Tavish stared back at him, his own lip curling. "And ye swill mead like an ale-house slattern."

This comment caused guffaws of laughter to ripple down the table. The two youngest brothers, Evan and Will, were engaged in a game of Ard-ri, while Blaine looked on, making derisive comments as each brother moved.

However, all three sniggered as Roy slumped back on the bench seat mumbling another insult.

Tavish ignored him. Instead, he leaned back on the clan-chief's carven chair—a chair his father had occupied until recently—and let his gaze sweep over the great hall. The Oliphants had all retired hours earlier, and only drunken warriors remained.

A servant approached the table then—a small, comely lass his father had tumbled a number of times. Gaze averted, she began to clear away the empty tankards and jugs. Her movements were deft and fast as if she wished to remain inconspicuous.

Unfortunately for her, she was not.

"Come here, bonny Jean." Roy lunged forward, grasped the serving wench around the waist, and hauled her onto his lap.

Jean's face went rigid. She tried to struggle, but Roy's thick arm held her fast.

"Now's yer chance, Tav," Roy slurred, groping the lass's breasts. "Yer last woman before ye shackle yerself with a wife."

Tavish heaved a sigh. Roy was wearisome at the best of times, although tonight his brother was really getting on his nerves. Ever since Tavish had stepped into the role of clan-chief, Roy had been sour when sober and boorish when in his cups.

"Ye don't want her?" Roy jeered, nuzzling Jean's neck. "Well, in that case, I might have a tumble ... all this talk of weddings makes my balls tight."

Snorts of mirth followed this comment, although Jean didn't look best pleased. Her blue eyes had gone as wide as moons, and she wore an expression of horror.

Tavish sucked in a deep breath before letting it out slowly. "That's enough, Roy. Let the lass be."

Roy lifted his head from Jean's neck and stared at his elder brother. His grey eyes were glazed and unfocused with drink, yet Tavish knew better than to underestimate him. All the brothers knew Roy was dangerous when drunk.

"I'm having her," he slurred, challenge in his voice.

"No, ye aren't. Father didn't mind ye groping the servants, Roy ... but I do."

Their father had deliberately chosen pretty women to work in his hall—and he'd swived his way through most of them.

"What's wrong with ye?" Roy countered, his mouth twisting. "I'm only taking what's owed to me after all."

"Ye are owed nothing." To make his point, Tavish drew the dirk he always carried at his hip and began to clean his nails with its wickedly pointed tip, focusing on that rather than Roy. "And if I have to repeat myself, blood will be spilled this night."

A dangerous quiet settled over the great hall at these words. Blaine, Evan, and Will had lost interest in the board game and were watching the interaction between their two elder brothers with interest.

Roy had made no secret of his resentment toward Tavish, or of his desire to be sitting in that chair, yet he usually minded his elder brother.

Would he tonight?

3
WIFELY DUTIES

"I MUST SPEAK to ye of yer wedding night, daughter." Isla Oliphant's voice held an eager edge that made Robina's belly clench. She'd known this 'talk' was coming and had dreaded it.

She'd been traumatized by her mother's conversations regarding intimate matters in the past and feared this occasion would be worse.

Standing in the midst of the chamber while Fiona, the maid who'd been assigned to her, laced up the back of her gown, Robina glanced her mother's way. *Must ye?*

She wished she could say the words, yet her mother had a quick temper and even quicker slap—and so she swallowed them.

Isla met her eye, her blue eyes gleaming. She then cleared her throat. "A wife has certain ... duties ... she must perform."

Robina went hot and then cold. "Aye ... Ma?"

She knew that. There had been occasions in the past when her mother, and her nurse, had spoken about the vile appetites of men. The servants at Kellie Castle, the Oliphant seat, had also often gossiped of indelicate matters. The snippets Robina had overheard had left her feeling queasy. After one such incident, she'd told her parents she wished to take the veil at Iona, yet her father had refused outright. "If I'm to pay a dowry for ye, Robina, it will be to make an alliance with one of our neighbors," he'd informed her. "Not to fatten the coffers of the church."

"Well ... on yer wedding night, ye must allow him to take his rights," her mother plowed on, "as a husband."

"Aye, Ma ... he will bed me."

Robina wasn't daft, she knew how bairns were made. She inwardly prayed her mother could cease this painful speech.

However, heedless, Isla Oliphant continued. "It will not be pleasurable, daughter, but ye must endure it, for that is a wife's lot."

Robina stared at her mother, not knowing how to answer, yet Lady Oliphant was not yet done.

"Carnal relations between husband and wife have just one purpose—to beget a bairn. I have given yer father four ... and although he takes his pleasure upon me whenever he wishes, I shall admit that I have never enjoyed it." She drew in a sharp breath then. "Prepare yerself, daughter, for an ordeal. On my wedding night, I felt as if I were being torn asunder. Now, it's true yer father is a 'big' man, but when he—"

"Ma!" Robina gasped, just as Fiona made a faint choking sound as if stifling a laugh. "That is sufficient. I need no further explanation."

Isla scowled. "I just want ye to be prepared, daughter."

"Well, now I am," Robina replied stiffly, her cheeks burning.

Had she imagined it, or had there been a vindictive edge to her mother's voice as she revealed those details? They'd never been close. Robina was the eldest child and three boys followed her—Isla's sons were her pride; she fussed over them, even now they were grown, in a way she never had over her husband or daughter.

Holding her mother's eye now, Robina realized the truth of it. Isla saw her daughter as a rival.

She was pleased Robina was marrying well for the sake of the clan, yet she didn't wish her well. She was enjoying frightening her.

A chill stole over Robina then, dousing the blush of embarrassment. Her mother's words just served to feed the fear that writhed in her belly. Her nurse had once told her that men were beasts in the marriage bed—that they enjoyed inflicting pain and embarrassment upon their wives. Murdina, who'd passed away the previous winter, had been a pious woman who'd never been wedded. Robina had wondered how her prudish nurse had gained such lurid details, yet her confusion hadn't eased the terror that had taken wing inside her at Murdina's words.

"There, Lady Robina." Fiona stepped back. "The gown is done ... shall we start on yer hair?"

"Aye," Robina murmured. She glanced down at her dark plum gown edged in gold then. She would wear a surcoat a shade darker on top of it.

Truthfully, she wished to send both her maid and mother from the chamber and lock the door behind them.

She felt as if she perched on the edge of a cliff with the sea roiling underneath her. She was clinging to the rocks by her fingertips, fighting the fall. But the plunge would come shortly, and there was no getting out of this.

"Leave my daughter's hair down," Isla instructed. "It flatters her face ... makes her complexion less sallow."

Robina's jaw clenched. How she dreaded her union to Tavish Gunn. Last night, he'd watched her during supper with the intensity of a hungry wolf. Frankly, the thought of becoming his wife made her feel as if she were going to the gallows. Nonetheless, as much as she didn't want to be here, she wouldn't miss being undermined by her mother.

"No," she said firmly, drawing her shoulders back. This was her wedding day, and she would decide how to wear her hair. They were away from Kellie Castle now, and already she could feel her mother's hold over her lessening. It filled her with unusual boldness. "Please put my hair up, Fiona." She flashed her mother a quelling look as she started to protest. "Use my amber combs."

The wind howled across the bailey, bringing with it flurries of snow. Standing upon the top step before the chapel, Tavish fought the urge to hunch his shoulders as he finished repeating the vows that would bind him and Robina Oliphant together.

All the while, he didn't take his gaze off her.

And unlike the day before when she'd been able to look elsewhere, Robina stared back.

Her hazel eyes were wide, startled. Snowflakes settled on her brown hair and upon the shoulders of the plush velvet surcoat she wore.

Even the freezing wind and threatening blizzard couldn't dim her loveliness.

Robina spoke her vows after him, her voice husky, with a slight nervous tremor. And she was nervous—he could virtually smell it on her.

It was understandable really—for the pair of them had spent little time together and shared few words. Yet Tavish wasn't apprehensive. He knew what he wanted— what he'd wanted since Robina Oliphant's first visit to Castle Gunn.

The ceremony concluded swiftly, for the wind was now blowing horizontally, causing tendrils to come free from Robina's intricately braided hair.

The chaplain was hunched in his dark robes like a crow, his beaky nose bright red.

Deftly, he unwound the strip of Gunn plaid that bound their joined hands. "Ye are now husband and wife," he muttered between chattering teeth.

Robina went to draw her hand away. Her fingers were slender and ice-cold, yet Tavish didn't relinquish his grip.

Instead, he squeezed gently before bending his head and brushing her lips with his.

Robina went rigid, and when Tavish pulled back, he saw that her eyes had gone wider still. Her elfin face had blanched.

It was only a kiss, yet she looked as if he'd just attempted to ravish her.

Pushing aside the unease that wreathed up at her reaction, Tavish turned his attention to the small knot of kin that had gathered to watch the ceremony.

"Hurry up!" his younger brother Will called. "My cods are freezing!"

This comment brought a censorious look from Lady Oliphant, even if her nose was as red as the chaplain's.

"It's done," Tavish called down to them. "Let us go into the great hall … where mulled wine and a great feast await us."

The well-wishers didn't need to be told twice. Cloaks flapping in the wind, they turned and hurried toward the keep. Castle Gunn's tiny chapel sat squeezed between the forge and the guard house.

Still holding his bride's hand, Tavish set off after them.

Snow swirled around them, creating a momentary veil of privacy between the couple.

Tavish glanced Robina's way. Her face was still taut, her jaw set as if she were readying herself for battle.

"Fear not, lass," he said, before flashing her a smile, "the worst is over with."

Robina's chin kicked up, her gaze glancing across his. The look he saw there made the uneasy sensation of earlier return, and his belly tensed. "Is it?" she rasped.

Seated at the table, cowed by the din inside the great hall of Castle Gunn, Robina reached for her goblet of wine.

Fingers fastening around the silver stem, she raised it to her lips and took a large gulp, and then another. The bramble wine warmed her belly, settling the writhing nerves.

~ 29 ~

I'm a wedded woman.

Robina swallowed hard before sneaking a glance at her husband's hawkish profile.

Not quite, she reminded herself. *There's still the wedding night to endure.*

Her jaw clenched. And endure it she must. As if it wasn't enough that her mother had succeeded in putting the fear of God into her when it came to losing her maidenhead, the thought of being intimate with a man she didn't want made resentment simmer within her.

I don't want this—any of it, she thought bitterly. *And I don't want him.*

Feeling her stare, Tavish Gunn stopped conversing with one of his brothers—the heavyset one with a thuggish face—and glanced her way.

Their gazes locked, and to her ire, the man's lips twitched.

"That's better," Gunn murmured. "If ye can meet yer husband's gaze without flinching, that's a start."

Heat flushed through Robina as sharp anger rose, an emotion that managed to settle nerves and shyness.

How tired she was of being treated as if she didn't matter. Farther down the table, her parents were digging into roast venison and making merry. The high-pitched trill of Isla Oliphant's laughter cut through the deep rumble of male voices around her.

And now Tavish Gunn was viewing her as if she were a skittish mare that needed to be broken.

Robina had had enough.

"If I avoid yer eye, I have my reasons," she replied. The wine made her bold, and she took another gulp to fortify herself. "I didn't wish to wed ye, Tavish Gunn ... although ye seem too dim-witted to notice that ... or to care."

Her words had been wielded like a filleting knife, and they had the desired effect, for all humor faded from the Gunn clan-chief's face.

Tavish Gunn was an attractive man—not in the chiseled way his elder brother had been—but he had hawkish, slightly wild looks that softened when he smiled. However, when his brows drew together as they did now, and those storm-grey eyes hooded, Robina was reminded that she had wed a Gunn—warriors that were both feared and hated by many.

"No woman should be forced to wed against her will," he said after a pause. "Had ye come to me yesterday and spoken to me thus, I would have respected yer wishes."

Robina fought a lip-curl. "Plenty of women wed when they wish not to," she growled back. "The law states one thing, but kin another." She paused then, casting a meaningful glance down the table to her father.

Ramsay Oliphant was in the process of draining his third goblet of wine, his cheeks flushed.

Ire writhed like a nest of vipers in her gut. Now that she'd let the beast out of the cage, it didn't want to go back in.

Swiveling her attention back to her husband, she found he was still staring at her. His face was expressionless, although his eyes had gone hard.

"My father has coveted an alliance with the Gunns for years," she continued, biting out the words. "He was bitterly disappointed when yer elder brother disgraced himself ... and vexed when yer father refused to speak of another marriage contract with ye or one of yer brothers." She paused then, her fingers tightening around the stem of her goblet. "It seems George Gunn was set upon me wedding Alexander."

Tavish Gunn's mouth thinned, his gaze narrowing. "Aye," he said roughly. "My brother never wanted ye though, Robina." He leaned forward then, his gaze never leaving hers. "Yet I do."

4

NOT YER ENEMY

HIS BRIDE'S HAZEL eyes flew wide, and Tavish had the brief satisfaction of seeing her delicate features stiffen with shock, the fire in her gaze dimming.

In contrast, his own kindled. The woman had just spoken to him like something she'd scraped off her shoe.

He felt duped. Where was the gentle-mannered lass he'd wed? He'd thought he was taking a demure, if timid, woman as his wife—not a scold.

Disappointment clenched within him, yet not as quickly as his rising temper. "Aye, that's right," he bit out. "Alexander fell in love with a Mackay … a wild, willful woman who stole his heart. He thought ye a meek mouse." Tavish broke off here, noting the way her slender jaw clenched. "But he was mistaken, wasn't he? Ye were just playing at being biddable and sweet."

His words were deliberately provocative, for underneath his anger and disappointment, Tavish was nursing a sharp embarrassment. Somehow this slender, elfin-faced woman had made a fool of him. He'd developed an infatuation with the image he'd formed of Robina Oliphant from a distance. And now she knew it.

The pair of them stared at each other for a long moment—a duel of wills. And as they did so, Tavish's temper gradually cooled.

No, this wasn't the gently-spoken woman he'd developed an obsession with from her first visit to Castle Gunn. Instead, his bride had spirit. It occurred to Tavish then that life with Robina would not be easy, yet could possibly end up more rewarding for it. She held his gaze with the intensity of one of her goshawks.

Excitement quickened in Tavish's gut, arousal tightening his groin. Suddenly, he wished this wedding banquet were over. The noise of the revelers and the coarse boom of Roy's laughter next to him faded.

The world became Robina's eyes—and as their stare drew out, he sensed a change in her.

His wife's breathing altered, her bosom lifting and falling in sharp movements, her soft pink lips parting.

Desire knifed through Tavish.

Aye, he couldn't wait till this wedding banquet was done.

What have I done?

Heart slamming against her ribs, Robina gazed into Tavish Gunn's eyes.

Her temper had gotten the better of her—and for a fleeting moment, a sense of power had thrummed through her.

She'd enjoyed shocking him, enjoyed seeing that arrogant smile fade.

But then he'd turned the tables on her.

And now he was looking at her like a hungry wolf—and she was his prey.

Judas, I'm a fool.

Blood roaring in her ears, Robina did tear her gaze from Tavish's. She was still reeling from his revelation. Before arriving at Castle Gunn, she'd thought he had agreed to wed her for political alliance, not because he 'wanted' her. Instead, all this time, he'd coveted her, even when he'd believed she'd been meant for his brother.

Even now, as she raised her goblet shakily to her lips, she could feel the heat of his gaze upon her. It scorched her.

Tavish Gunn didn't need to say a word: one look at his tight expression, his burning eyes, told her that he lusted after her. Inadvertently, she'd stoked that lust with her shrewish words.

She'd wanted to wound, to put him off, and yet it had had the opposite effect.

Robina took another large gulp of wine.

The saints preserve her, how was she supposed to survive her wedding night?

The wedding banquet was over too quickly. The food stuck in Robina's throat, the wine had gone straight to her head, and she'd broken out in a cold sweat—yet no one noticed or cared.

The music grew louder, as did the raucous laughter and singing. Queasiness stole over Robina, and when the tables below the dais were pushed back and couples took to the floor, fear clamped her belly.

She didn't want to dance with her husband.

And yet she had no choice.

Tavish rose from his seat, took her hand, and led his bride out onto the floor. The strength and heat of his hand engulfing hers only served to make Robina's galloping pulse race even faster.

The lyre played a gentle melody, and the couple settled into a *basse danse*, a courtly dance in which they circled each other.

Robina wasn't a confident dancer—she'd always been too shy to truly enjoy it. And it made her feel like a prize filly, parading in front of potential suitors for her parents' benefit.

Laird and Lady Oliphant sat upon the dais, faces flushed with wine. The self-important expression on her father's face and the smug look upon her mother's made bitterness sour Robina's mouth.

They'd sold her off to the Gunns without a thought to her happiness.

Tavish Gunn's father, George Gunn's, cruelty and brutality were legend throughout the Highlands. Did they think his sons weren't cast in the same mold?

Maybe they did, but they didn't care.

As she went through the motions of the dance, taking care to avoid her husband's wolfish gaze, Robina spied his brothers. The loutish one now had a serving lass upon his lap. Grinning, he groped the young woman's breasts while she squirmed and tried to get away.

Robina suppressed a shudder. Roy Gunn was a pig. Catching her looking in his direction, Roy's grin widened. The man then had the audacity to lift his tankard of ale to her, with the hand he wasn't using to molest the serving lass, in a mocking salute.

Jaw clenched, Robina looked away.

The dance came to an end, and husband and wife bestowed each other with a formal bow.

Not waiting for the music to recommence, Robina fled back to her seat.

Moments later, Tavish joined her. "I take it ye aren't fond of dancing?" he asked, wry amusement lacing his voice.

"No," she replied, her own tone clipped. "I find I have little aptitude for it."

Tavish quirked a dark eyebrow. "Ye seemed perfectly graceful to me."

Robina glared at him, searching for mockery in his eyes. However, she saw none.

Their stare drew out, and then Tavish shook his head. "Ye give me an ill-favored look, Robina. I'm yer husband, not yer enemy."

Robina stiffened, yet she managed to swallow the words that clawed up her throat, desperate to spill out. She wasn't sure what was wrong with her this evening; it was as if a lifetime of resentment had just come to the boil—and now it surged up, seeking release.

All those things she'd wanted to say to her parents over the years—but hadn't—now surged within her.

Tavish inclined his head. "Ye are angry, wife. Does my presence vex ye so?"

Robina drew in a deep, steadying breath as she attempted to calm the storm within her. She needed to get ahold of herself—to put her anger back in its cage.

Raging at the man who was now her husband wouldn't help matters. When it came to the bedding, he'd just be even more brutal. Her mother had told her once that it was no good trying to deny a man his base carnal needs. He'd only take what he wanted in the end after he'd hurt her all the more.

"It's not just ye," she said eventually, her voice rough with the force of the emotions churning within her. "It's everything."

He raised his eyebrows, inviting her to continue.

Robina sucked in another breath. She really didn't want to confide in this man, for she didn't like or trust him—and yet the loneliness of her existence, the fact that there was no one she could confide in, was getting too much. Suddenly, she felt so terribly alone; she felt that there wasn't a soul alive who cared how she felt.

"My wants have never mattered," she admitted after a pause, her voice husky. "To my kin, I'm just something to be used to foster an alliance between our clans." She heaved in a shaky breath, aware that she was now raving but unable to stop herself. "When I told my father that I didn't wish to wed, it was as if one of our fowls had just informed them that it no longer wanted to lay eggs. He made it clear that my only purpose was to help our clan prosper. What else are daughters good for?" Her voice trailed off as heat swept over her. Embarrassed and aware that her cheeks now flamed, Robina dropped her gaze to the goblet she clutched.

Wretchedness clenched within her. What in the devil was she doing confiding such things to Tavish Gunn? He would think her a mewling wench.

Tensing, she waited for his scorn, his derision. Yet none came.

Long moments passed, and then Robina glanced up. Tavish Gunn was still watching her—and yet there was no sneer upon his face, no disdain or mockery in his eyes.

Instead, his mouth lifted at the edges, even as he continued to hold her gaze. "Yer wants matter to me," he said softly.

5

TIME FOR THE BEDDING

ROBINA DIDN'T KNOW what to say to that.

Her first reaction was disbelief. How could she matter to him? He didn't even know her. Moments passed, and then a chill settled in her belly. Was he patronizing her?

"I mean it," Tavish continued, his voice low, as if he was ensuring no one overheard them. "I've wanted ye for years, Robina. We are but strangers still … yet I wish to change that."

Heat flushed over Robina, dousing the chill.

There was an intimacy to his voice that embarrassed her. She'd gone and done it now—had dug a hole for herself. She'd wanted to keep herself walled off from her Gunn husband, and yet the opposite had happened.

Robina glanced down at her goblet of wine—it was nearly empty. Had Tavish added some potent herb to it, to addle her wits?

Fingers clenching around the stem, Robina dismissed the notion. No, she couldn't blame Gunn for this. Her outburst, the tide of details her husband had never asked for, had flowed out of her tonight.

"Time for the bedding," Roy slurred then, his voice intruding. Shifting her gaze across to Tavish's brother, she saw the brute still had the hapless serving lass upon his lap. The poor woman's eyes were wild with panic as he continued to paw at her ripe breasts with one hand—delving under her skirts with the other.

"Come on, brother," Roy continued with a leer. Farther down the table, the three younger brothers—Blaine, Evan, and William—were now grinning like idiots. All gazes were upon the wedded couple. "What's wrong ... afraid ye are not up to the task?" Roy cast Robina a lingering look. "I can bed yer wife instead, if ye like?"

Robina's stomach lurched at the suggestion. Roy's younger brothers laughed, although no one else at the table—her parents included—showed any mirth.

And neither did Tavish.

Placing his goblet on the table before him, her husband's gaze raked over his brother as if taking his measure. An instant later, his lip curled. "I can bed my own wife, thank ye, Roy," he replied, his tone cool. "And I've warned ye before about groping that poor lass." Tavish met the young woman's eye before nodding. "Off ye go, Jean."

Relief suffused the lass's face. She twisted out of Roy's grip and scrambled from his lap before hurrying off in the direction of the kitchens.

Silence fell over the table, and Roy's face went the color of raw meat.

His expression then screwed up, and he spat upon the dais, between him and Tavish. "My brother," he snarled. "The priest."

Tavish fastened him with a humorless smile. "No ... yer brother ... the clan-chief." He reached out and took Robina by the hand, guiding her to her feet. His gaze then shifted down the table to Robina's parents. Ramsay and Isla Oliphant had been viewing the exchange between the brothers with keen interest.

As had everyone else at the table.

"We shall bid ye all a good night," Tavish announced. "Please continue to make merry ... and we shall see ye on the morrow."

Tavish's fingers tightened, just a little, around Robina's then, and her heart quailed.

Mother Mary, it was about to happen—the bedding.

Tavish led Robina from the great hall, amidst a chorus of drunken, ribald calls. Face flaming, Robina kept her gaze fixed firmly on the door. And although she'd been dreading the moment she and her husband would finally be alone, a strange relief swept over her when the heavy door thudded shut behind them and they were making their way up the spiral staircase to the floors above.

"I must apologize for my brother," Tavish said after a pause. He still held her hand, his grip both firm and yielding. "He oftentimes forgets himself ... especially when he's had a skinful."

Robina didn't reply. All the same, her feelings toward Roy must have shown on her face, for Tavish's hawkish features tensed. "Don't worry, I'll ensure he minds his tongue around ye in future."

Robina's mouth pursed. "He resents ye, doesn't he? Roy wishes he were clan-chief."

Tavish snorted a laugh. They were approaching the top landing now, the light from the cressets upon the walls gilding the proud lines of his face. "Aye ... it's always galled him that he was the third-born son ... and not the first."

"And yet, with yer eldest brother gone from Castle Gunn, Roy is next in line should anything happen to ye."

Tavish cocked a dark eyebrow. "Ye think he'll try to rid himself of me?"

Robina could hear the wry edge to his tone, although her own gaze remained serious. "Perhaps ... ye should be wary of him."

Their gazes fused, and then Tavish's mouth quirked. "Fear not ... I already am."

The chaplain was waiting for them. Entering the large chamber through the clan-chief's solar, Robina tried to slow the panicked beating of her heart by taking deep, measured breaths.

However, at the sight of the chaplain standing before the biggest bed she'd ever seen, Robina's belly churned and bile stung the back of her throat.

Lord, how will I weather this?

The chaplain blessed the bed, sprinkling holy water over the coverlet, before murmuring a blessing over Tavish and Robina as they perched, side-by-side, upon the edge of the bed.

The blessing was spoken quickly, and then the chaplain left, the door whispering shut behind him.

Robina drew in a deep breath as her pulse now thundered in her ears. The time had come—and she wasn't ready. She doubted she ever would be. Long moments stretched out as she and Tavish continued to sit in silence. And with each passing moment, Robina's panic grew.

Tavish reached out then, covering her hand with his. "I meant what I said earlier," he murmured, his voice a low rumble. "Ye matter to me, Robina ... long have I wished to make ye my wife."

Robina realized he'd only said such to allay her fears—however, his words merely made her break out in a cold sweat.

Tavish Gunn might have made the decision to wed her, yet Robina felt as if she'd been bullied, pushed, and guilted into this position.

Ma says it will hurt.

She recalled Isla Oliphant's words earlier in the day—and the glint in her gaze as she'd uttered them. Her mother had enjoyed scaring her daughter, and not for the first time over the years. Together, Isla and Murdina had created a terrifying impression of what happened between a man and woman.

Robina closed her eyes.

She just wanted it to be over.

Tavish's fingers hooked gently under her chin then, and he angled her face toward him. Robina's eyes flickered open, her heart quailing when she saw the hunger in his storm-grey eyes. And then, without another word, he leaned in and kissed her.

His lips brushed across Robina's, feather-light at first, as he judged her reaction. And then he kissed her again, his hands gently clasping her shoulders as he drew her into his embrace.

And despite that she was terrified, despite that her heart was beating so fast she felt as if it would leap from her chest, she noted the pleasant smell of him: a blend of wood smoke, wine, and the male musk of his skin.

His lips brushed across hers once more, and then his tongue gently parted them.

Robina froze, panic flaring like a fiery beacon within her breast.

Lord, no!

"Just relax, mo chridhe," Tavish murmured. "Let yerself enjoy it."

My Heart. The endearment didn't soothe Robina; instead, it just unsettled her further. She couldn't enjoy it—not when she knew what it would lead to.

Even so, if she sprang away from him, things would only get worse for her.

Robina's mother had lectured her endlessly on how a wife should obey her husband in all things. And so, Robina would have to suffer Tavish Gunn's kiss.

Cupping her face with his hands, he kissed her again, his tongue sliding against hers in a gentle, languorous rhythm.

And, curse her, she found herself liking the taste of him. He had a way of kissing—both gentle and passionate—that caused a kernel of heat to ignite in her belly, like a tender flame. He cupped her face with his hands with reverence, as if he held something delicate and precious.

Robina's heart still drummed against her ribs, sweat now bathing her limbs, yet his gentle approach, his sensual mouth, kept the panic within her from bubbling up, from spilling over.

And then one of his hands slid to the back of her head, possessively cradling it as he deepened the kiss. The tender flame within Robina flared brightly for an instant, as the heat of Tavish's desire washed over her.

But when a low groan issued from his throat and he drew her toward him—that flame sputtered and went out.

Ice-cold fear flooded through Robina's veins. Her body went rigid, and she tore herself away from him, tumbling off the edge of the bed in her effort to flee from her husband's side.

Hitting the cold flagstones, Robina scrambled backward before cringing against the wall.

And all the while, she never took her gaze from Tavish, lest he leap at her.

Breathing hard, Robina lifted a hand to her lips, still tingling from his kisses. It was no good—she'd tried to force herself to go through with this—to do her duty.

But she couldn't.

If Tavish touched her again, she'd screech and claw at him like a hell-cat.

"Robina?" The horror on her husband's face, the shock in his eyes, barely penetrated Robina's crippling panic. "What is it? What's wrong?"

"Everything," she gasped, her voice catching in her throat. "I can't do this ... please don't make me."

6

TAVISH'S PLEDGE

TAVISH STARED AT his wife as if she'd just transformed into something else entirely. Not a comely woman with a sweet-tasting mouth and soft lips that begged to be kissed—but a wild, panicked animal that cringed away from him.

In an instant, the lust that had heated Tavish's blood cooled, and the erection that had been pressing almost painfully against the tight leather trews he wore tonight eased.

The terror in Robina's eyes was sobering indeed—only Tavish didn't understand what had caused it.

"I don't understand, Robina," he murmured, gentling his voice, as he did when dealing with a frightened horse. "Why do ye fear me?"

Her large eyes gleamed with unshed tears. "I don't want ye to hurt me."

Tavish stilled. "*Hurt* ye? Why would ye think I'd do that?"

Robina wrapped her arms around her slender frame. "Ye wouldn't be able to help yerself ... ye are a man after all."

Tavish frowned. He was truly struggling to comprehend the woman. None of this made any sense. She seemed to believe he was going to brutalize her.

"I promise nothing of the kind would happen," he said after a pause. "Have I not been gentle till now?"

She shook her head, denying his words. "Only to draw me into yer net ... to get me to trust ye." A shudder went through her then. "But I know what comes after."

Tavish raised an eyebrow. "Ye do?"

"Aye ... and I do not wish to be treated that way ... to be hurt and humiliated."

Heat washed over Tavish—a mixture of horror and rising anger. "I don't know what manner of beast ye believe me to be, Robina, but I would never do either of those things to ye." He paused then, seeking to rein in his reaction. He didn't want to frighten her further. Gentling his voice, he continued, "A woman's first time can be ... uncomfortable ... yet only her first. After that, it can be very pleasurable ... for *both* parties."

Robina stared back at him, her features taut with fear. "I don't believe ye," she rasped. "That's a lie." Her voice cracked then, and Tavish's anger dimmed.

Satan's cods, the lass thought that coupling meant agony for the woman. Who had led her to believe such things?

Terror pulsed from her, so potent he could almost taste it.

Slowly, so as not to scare her further, Tavish slid off the bed, sinking onto the floor so that their gazes were level.

Robina tracked him, her body coiling as if she thought he might pounce on her.

Something deep in Tavish's chest twisted. He couldn't help it—he was bitterly disappointed. He'd been looking forward to this day—this night—for months, yet his bride abhorred his touch.

Stubborn determination welled within him then. This was a setback—a large one—but he couldn't let this shaky start ruin his marriage. He couldn't continue to let Robina gaze upon him with fear shadowing her eyes.

This had to be nipped in the bud, right from the beginning.

Slowly, he slid forward so that they were around two feet apart—close enough that he could reach out and touch her.

"Give me yer hand, Robina," he murmured. When she didn't move, he swallowed. "Please ... I won't harm ye."

A nerve flickered in her jaw, a little of the fire he'd seen during the wedding banquet resurfacing. Moments passed before she slowly reached out a trembling hand toward him.

Tavish took it, his fingers folding gently over hers.

"I know ye weren't keen on this marriage," he said, his voice low, "But I'd hoped ye would warm to me all the same." He paused then, seeking the right words, ones that wouldn't alarm her. "Ye need never fear me, Robina. I solemnly make ye a pledge this night ... that I will always treat ye gently ... that I will treasure yer body." His gaze held hers fast. "One day, when ye are ready, I will show ye how it should be when a man takes his wife ... but I am prepared to wait."

Robina stared back at him, her face pale, her jaw tense.

"All that I ask in return," Tavish continued, cupping their joined hands with his free one, "is that ye trust me enough to believe that I mean ye no harm." He could feel her pulse racing under his fingertips yet pressed on. "I wish ye to share my bed tonight." Alarm flared in her eyes, and she tried to pull away, yet his grip remained firm, as did his gaze. "I swear to ye ... I will not touch ye, yet there will never be any trust between us if ye don't let me prove myself to ye," he murmured. "Ye have my word that I will not overstep ... however, I need yers that ye will meet me halfway." He paused then, letting the moment draw out. "Will ye?"

Silence fell between them. Far below, Tavish could hear the muffled sound of music and laughter. Oblivious to the turmoil within his chamber, their guests and kin continued to make merry.

Long moments passed, and then, just when Tavish began to believe he'd pushed things too far, Robina nodded.

Robina stirred in the bed, coming awake slowly. For a few blessed instants, she imagined she was back home, in her old bed—and then she remembered.

Castle Gunn.

The wedding ceremony.

The banquet.

The terror that had pulsed through her as she'd cringed away from her husband.

Eyes flickering open, Robina tensed. She lay facing the wall, yet sensed she was not alone in the bed. Heat fluttering at the base of her throat, she remained there, wondering at her next move.

Her husband's deep, even breathing filled the bed-chamber. Tavish was still asleep.

Carefully, so she didn't wake him, Robina rolled over, her gaze alighting on Tavish's sleeping face.

He lay on his side, facing her, his sharp features soft in repose.

Robina continued to watch him, her gaze shifting to where one naked arm lay on top of the blankets. To her relief, although he'd stripped off his lèine and vest, he'd left his trews on.

It had been painfully awkward, those moments after she'd agreed to trust him, yet they'd both managed to ready themselves for bed and climb in without another scene erupting.

Robina had undressed behind a screen in a corner of the bed-chamber before donning a night-rail and woolen robe. She'd then emerged and darted across the room before diving under the covers—careful to keep to her side of the bed.

"Goodnight, Robina," Tavish had murmured, a note of dry humor in his voice.

"Goodnight," she'd replied stiffly.

And that was it—the last words between them before dawn the following morning.

There was a little light in the bed-chamber, for the brick of peat in the hearth still burned low and watery light filtered into the room through a gap in the shutters—enough light to allow Robina to study he husband's sleeping face.

She was relieved he wasn't yet awake—for she was embarrassed in the aftermath of the night before. She couldn't believe she'd lost control like that. Fear had turned her witless, yet Tavish had somehow managed to calm her.

And he'd remained true to his word—he'd 'let her be' overnight. He hadn't touched her.

Robina's belly tightened. How long would it be before he pushed the boundaries with her?

He'd made her a pledge, yet would he keep it?

Tavish stirred then, his long, lean body stretching. His eyes fluttered open. They were a little unfocused from sleep, yet they sharpened when he saw that she was watching him.

"Good morn, wife," he greeted her, his voice a little gravelly. "Did ye sleep well?"

Watching her parents depart, Robina felt nothing but a wave of relief. Her mother had observed her like a hawk all morning—and had even asked her how the bedding went.

Robina had ignored her, pretending not to hear.

She wouldn't answer Isla Oliphant's prying questions: not now, not ever. The things her mother had told her about coupling, about the agony it put a woman through, still plagued her. A few times, she caught her mother scrutinizing her face as if searching for a sign of trauma.

Robina would give her nothing.

"Our Robina will give ye plenty of strapping sons," her father boomed as he slapped Tavish on the back. They stood in the bailey, snow fluttering down from a colorless sky. "I expect to hear by spring that she is with bairn ... as well as news about leasing the grazing land we spoke of."

Tavish grunted at this comment before stepping back next to Robina.

"Safe travels home," he said, his voice bland.

"It'll be slow ... with this damned snow," Isla Ramsay sniffed. "I was hoping ye would invite us to stay for Yuletide ... as would have been proper."

Tavish favored Lady Oliphant with a cool smile. "It would have been my pleasure, but as I have kin arriving for the festive season, there will not be enough bed-chambers to accommodate ye all."

"But *we* are family now," Isla informed him imperiously. She sat atop her courser, shrouded in furs, her long face sharp with disapproval.

"Aye, Lady Oliphant," Tavish replied smoothly, "yet blood kin always takes precedence, does it not?"

"Aye," Robina's father answered heartily, swinging up onto his mount. "Of course it does. Stop whining, Isla."

Lady Oliphant's cheeks colored at this, her lips thinning, yet she minded her husband.

Robina lifted a hand in farewell as the Oliphant party turned and crossed the bailey toward the raised portcullis and the rickety wooden bridge beyond.

"Do ye really have kin visiting for Yule?" she asked Tavish softly, her gaze never leaving her parents retreating backs.

"No," Tavish replied.

Robina glanced his way to see that her husband wore a half-smile, his eyes glinting. "But I've had enough of their company," he continued, "as I wager have ye."

7
MEETING IN THE MEWS

"FIONA, MAY I ask ye something ... something personal?"

"Aye, Lady Robina." The maid glanced up from where she was sorting through a box of combs and hair pins. "Of course."

Robina shifted uncomfortably upon her chair. She'd been on edge all morning since her parents' departure. She wouldn't miss them—Tavish had been right about that, although she wasn't about to admit so to him.

In truth, his blunt comment had made her even more ill at ease in his presence.

She wasn't used to being seen, noticed.

Robina glanced up to see her maid was waiting for her to voice her question. Embarrassment suddenly swept through Robina, and yet—seeing the frank look on the lass's eyes—she forced herself to speak.

"It's about what happens" —Robina cleared her throat— "between husband and wife."

Fiona stilled before her eyes widened. "Aye ... and?"

"Have ye ever lain with a man, Fiona?"

The maid's cheeks went a delicate shade of pink.

"Fear not ... I won't tell anyone," Robina added hastily, heat rising to her own face. "It's just that I wish to know what happens ... and how much it actually hurts."

Fiona's features tightened, her gaze roaming over Robina's face. "Ye didn't lie with yer husband last night then?"

Robina shook her head. "I panicked ..."

Fiona made a sound of disbelief in the back of her throat. "Surely, ye don't believe what yer mother told ye yesterday, Lady Robina?"

Robina frowned. "My mother isn't the only one who has said such ... my nurse also warned me about men's beastly ways." Her frown deepened. "Why would either of them lie about something so important?"

Fiona took a step closer, her gaze shadowing with concern. "If I may speak plainly, Lady Robina, I found the things yer mother said to ye to be ... unfounded."

Robina's frown turned into a scowl. "So, it isn't agony?"

Fiona shook her head. "The first time can bring ye a little discomfort ... for a moment or two ... but then" —a smile stretched her face— "it becomes immensely pleasurable."

Robina stilled. "Pleasurable?" She said stupidly.

Fiona's smile widened. "Aye ... if a man knows what he's about, he can give a woman as much pleasure as he takes."

"And ye have met such a man?" Robina was both aghast and intrigued.

A blush bloomed once more across Fiona's cheeks. "Aye ... Malcolm ... the castle's austringer."

Robina stared back at her maid, concern bubbling up inside her. Why would any woman voluntarily lie with a man, if the experience was as traumatic as her mother and nurse had led her to believe?

Seeing the look on her mistress's face, Fiona huffed a laugh. "Have I scandalized ye, Lady Robina?"

Robina shook her head, although the truth was that her maid's words had sent her into turmoil.

The women's gazes met and held for a few moments before Fiona inclined her head. "Ye could do far worse than Tavish Gunn as a husband, my lady." Fiona's expression changed then, her eyes developing a mischievous glint. "And I've heard from one of the chambermaids, who once had an 'encounter' with him ... that the laird knows his way around a woman's body."

Robina's face was still glowing like a beacon when she left the women's solar.

The Lord preserve her, she'd never had a more embarrassing conversation.

Fiona's frank speech, and the way she so eagerly imparted intimate details, made Robina blush right down to the tip of her toes.

So her husband had once bedded servants, had he? Heat rolled through Robina once more. He'd told his brother off the night before, but was he really any different?

Robina's mouth thinned. *Beasts ... all of them.*

Upon the landing outside the solar, she found Misty, the Highland Collie, waiting for her. The dog rose stiffly to her feet and approached Robina, tail wagging.

"Good morning, lass." Robina ruffled her fluffy head and ears. "I'm going up to the mews. Do ye wish to join me?"

The dog leaned into her leg, and for a moment, Robina forgot her embarrassment, her confusion. The collie's uncomplicated affection soothed her.

Robina gave Misty's side a stroke before leading the way up the stairs toward the roof of the keep. Tavish had told her that the mews was located up here—and she longed to see her two goshawks. She'd been so distracted by the wedding that she hadn't visited Moth and Thistle since her arrival at Castle Gunn. She was irritated with herself now, for she should have at least checked earlier to make sure their lodgings were suitable.

The mews at Kellie Castle was a stone building in the outer ward—yet the setup at Castle Gunn appeared to be quite different.

At the top of the stairs, Robina pushed open a heavy wooden door to the outside before climbing another set of stairs—these slippery with ice and snow. Misty still padded behind her, and woman and dog emerged onto the castle roof.

Drawing her fur-lined clock about her, Robina breathed in the gelid air while her gaze scanned the crenelated wall that lined the space.

It had stopped snowing for a spell, and the sky had lightened. Moving to the ramparts, Robina surveyed the panorama before her.

She'd never liked Castle Gunn—had always found it a bleak, soulless place—but she had to admit that the view from this height was breathtaking. She just had to ensure she didn't move too close to the edge and look directly down.

To the east, the sea glittered silver in the weak winter sun, while to the west, ivory hills, so pristine white they almost hurt the eyes, rolled into a hazy horizon.

Robina heaved a sigh. Aye, it was beautiful—yet a cold, stark beauty all the same.

Turning, she crunched across the snow to the squat stone building that sat on the eastern edge of the roof. Robina paused before the door and cast a look over her shoulder. Misty had halted and was viewing her expectantly.

"Best ye remain here, lass," she murmured. "Ye might make the birds nervous."

The collie sat down, soft brown gaze imploring.

Smiling, Robina turned back to the door, knocked briefly, and then entered.

Stepping into a dimly lit interior, the air sharp with the odor of bird droppings, Robina's gaze went to the brazier that glowed a foot away.

A young man stood there, warming his hands over the glowing coals.

He glanced up, his blue eyes widening at the sight of her.

Robina favored him with a tight smile. "Ye must be Malcolm," she greeted him.

The austringer—the keeper of the Gunn's hawks—nodded. "Good morning, Lady Robina." He offered her a smile then, his youthful face turning handsome in an instant. "It's a cold morning to pay the mews a visit."

Robina stood there a moment, embarrassment warring with the need to spend time with her hawks. Knowing that this man was her maid's lover made her uncomfortable, yet the austringer had no idea that Fiona had confided in her mistress.

"Aye," she replied, noting how her breath steamed indoors despite the brazier. "But I wanted to see how my goshawks are settling in."

Malcolm's smile widened. Stepping back from the brazier, he adjusted the heavy fur around his shoulders before motioning to the row of partitioned spaces that covered two walls of the mews.

There, sharing a partition and tethered to a perch, sat Moth and Thistle.

A wide smile bloomed across Robina's face at the sight of them, and for an instant, she forgot her discomfort. "Good morn, my lovelies," she murmured. Approaching the two goshawks, she whispered other endearments to them before reaching out and stroking their feathered necks and backs with the back of her hand.

"It takes a brave soul to do that, Lady Robina," Malcolm murmured from behind her. "Those beaks can do serious damage."

"Moth and Thistle won't harm me," Robina replied. "My father's austringer stole them from a nest when they were tiny. He took them too young, and they nearly died … so I raised them … trained them."

A draft of chill air gusted into the mews then—with the opening of the door behind her. Robina glanced over her shoulder, going rigid when she spied her husband's lean form. Encased in leather, a fur mantle about his shoulders, and his long dark hair fastened at the nape— Tavish Gunn had the same predatory look as the birds of prey housed within the mews.

"Laird," Malcolm greeted him, surprise lacing his voice. "I wasn't expecting—"

"It's all right, Malcolm," Tavish replied with an aloof smile, even if his gaze remained upon Robina. "I was looking for my wife."

"And ye have found her," Robina replied. She turned back to her goshawks, frustration curling like smoke within her. *Can't he give me a moment alone?*

Tensing, she heard the tread of his boots on the stone floor, and then Tavish stood at her shoulder.

"They are bonny hawks," he murmured, "although it surprises me ye own two ... training just one hawk to hunt and return to yer wrist is quite some work."

"Moth and Thistle are sisters ... I didn't want to separate them." She paused then and cut him a glance. "Do ye hawk?"

Tavish nodded before gesturing to one of the partitions farther along the wall. "The sparrow hawk is mine."

Robina shifted her attention to where a male hawk perched watching her with gleaming black and amber eyes. It was a beautiful bird with blue-grey features upon its back and wings, and a rust-colored belly and lower face.

"Don't let his small stature fool ye," Tavish continued. "Reaper is the best hunter in the mews."

"Aye," Malcolm agreed from behind him. "He's been known to take down prey twice his own size."

Robina suppressed a snort. Men and their propensity for boasting. Everything was a competition.

"Both Moth and Thistle are able hunters," she replied, glancing back at her goshawks. They were both larger than Reaper—with mackerel bellies, walnut-colored wings, and a distinctive white arrow above each eye.

"We shall have to ride out for a spot of hawking soon then," Tavish replied, "as soon as the snow melts."

Robina nodded, a kernel of warmth igniting within her. She was pleased her husband liked hawking. The sport had been her escape, her solace, over the years.

"I haven't yet exercised yer birds today, Lady Robina," Malcolm said, interrupting their conversation. "If ye'd like to take them out onto the roof?"

Robina glanced over her shoulder at the austringer. She didn't like the idea of exercising the birds up here. Her dislike of heights meant she wouldn't be able to relax. "Ye don't have a weathering yard?"

"No, Robina," Tavish answered before Malcolm had a chance. "We let our hawks fly from the roof." There was a challenge in his voice as he continued. "Hopefully, yer birds are well-trained enough to return to yer glove?"

Robina's mouth thinned as she rose to the bait. She swiveled back to her husband, meeting his eye. "They are."

8

MY WIFE, NOT MY PRISONER

THE CHILL AIR bit at Robina's face when she stepped back out onto the roof, one arm aloft. She wore a leather hawking glove—upon which Moth sat, leashed to her wrist by a thin leather hunting jess.

Behind her, Tavish followed, with Thistle perched upon his right wrist. Wordlessly, the pair of them crunched across the snow, past where Misty now lay watching them, to the crenelated wall.

Making sure to stay well back from the edge, Robina waited until Tavish had stopped at her shoulder before glancing his way. "Ready?"

"Aye." He flashed her a grin. "Let these ladies fly."

They loosed the hawks' jesses, and an instant later, both birds took off, flying high into the winter sky.

Robina watched them, craning her neck as Moth and Thistle dived and soared.

"Ye adore them, don't ye?" Tavish observed, a teasing edge to his voice.

"Aye," Robina replied, not taking her gaze from the sky. "They make me feel ... free."

Silence stretched between them before Tavish answered, "Ye aren't caged, Robina."

Tensing, she forced herself to look at him. "Aren't I?"

He held her gaze, his expression more solemn than she'd yet seen it. "No ... ye are my wife, not my prisoner. Ye have the freedom to wander this keep at will ... and beyond if ye wish." He paused then, his gaze narrowing. "All I ask is that ye cease looking at me as yer dungeon master ... or as if I'm about to rape ye."

Heat rose to Robina's cheeks then. She'd been so focused on her goshawks that she'd almost forgotten her conversation with Fiona earlier that morning and the acute embarrassment that followed it.

Pleasurable.

That was the word her maid had used to describe the union between a man and woman. And then, heedless to her mistress's burning cheeks, the maid had gone on to explain, in great detail, how the act actually worked.

Recalling the description, Robina swallowed. She really didn't want to blush again, to give herself away.

Now that Tavish held her eye once more, the details her maid had imparted made her feel a trifle breathless and giddy.

It's my empty belly, she told herself. Indeed, she hadn't eaten since the night before.

"Ye already promised ye wouldn't ravish me," she said huskily.

"Aye." He stepped closer before reaching up with his ungloved hand. "I'm not the kind of man to take a woman against her will."

Robina tensed, forcing herself not to shrink back. Tavish's hand hesitated, his gaze shadowing before he drew it away. "I was only going to stroke yer cheek, Robina. There's no need to pull away from me as if I'm a leper."

Swallowing, Robina stepped back from him. His nearness was disconcerting, confusing.

She glanced away, following the path of her goshawks as they swooped overhead.

"I've lived a sheltered life, Tavish," she said softly, realizing that it was the first time she'd addressed her husband by his Christian name. "More so than I realized." When he didn't answer, she continued. "I have no sisters or female cousins or aunts ... my mother and nurse were my only source of conversation and advice" —she swallowed hard— "on certain matters."

She looked over at Tavish, who was observing her, a nonplussed expression on his face. No doubt, he was wondering what her point was.

She had to enlighten him.

Heart pounding, Robina severed eye contact with him once more. "My mother told me that marriage is a trial ... that a woman will only ever find pain and discomfort in the marriage bed."

Her husband's smoky gaze snapped wide. "Why the devil would she say that?" Tavish asked, his tone hardening.

"I don't know ... bitterness ... vindictiveness perhaps," Robina replied, something twisting deep within her chest. In truth, she had no idea why her mother would wish to scare her so. She'd always been competitive with her only daughter, yet this seemed a step too far.

"Surely, ye would have heard views contrary to hers though ... from servants?"

Robina shook her head, still not looking his way. "My nurse was a pious woman with very stern opinions on morality. She'd never wed and had never wanted to." Her voice died off there, embarrassment flushing through her. "And she often warned me of the 'vile appetites' of men."

She wasn't sure why she'd spoken honestly to Tavish—she'd never been this frank with anyone.

However, strangely, coming to live at Castle Gunn had unleashed something in her. Her husband was an arrogant warrior, yet being in his presence made honesty flow out of her—like an icicle melting after a long, cold winter freeze.

"So that's why ye were so frightened of me last night," Tavish said after a pause. "Yer mother and nurse put the fear of God into ye."

Robina nodded once more.

Another silence stretched between them then before Tavish spoke, a husky edge to his voice, "Please, look at me, Robina."

Steeling herself, Robina turned to him. She'd expected to see annoyance or frustration tightening his features—yet she didn't. Instead, he was watching her with a look of concern, his gaze shadowed.

"I must admit, I'm in new territory with all this," he said, offering her a tight smile. "The past day has taught me how little I know of women."

Robina snorted a laugh then—she couldn't help it, for his candor caught her off guard. "At least ye admit it." She replied, a smile tugging at her lips. "Most men wouldn't."

He stepped toward her, and this time, she didn't shrink back. "I lost my mother young and have no sisters. With a dominant father and five aggressive brothers, I've only ever lived in a man's world."

Robina met Tavish's eye. Once again, his honesty surprised her. But this time, she didn't laugh. "Ye are a man of many contradictions, Tavish Gunn," she murmured. "I don't know what to make of ye."

He cocked a dark eyebrow. "And I am completely baffled by ye, lass." He smiled then. "But we have time ... to put all of that right."

Robina's belly fluttered. A strange, yet not unpleasant, sensation.

Their gazes held for a moment longer, and then Tavish looked away, digging into the pouch Malcolm had handed him before they went outside. He extracted two chunks of meat—from rodents the austringer trapped for his birds—and handed one to Robina.

"Let's put Moth and Thistle back on their perches and go inside," he murmured. "The noon meal approaches ... and I think we could do with some mulled wine."

Robina smiled back, taking the meat from him and holding her gloved hand up. She adored mulled wine—a special treat at this time of year, with costly spices such as cinnamon and cloves added. "I'd like that," she murmured. Then she let out a shrill whistle, calling to her goshawks.

Moth plummeted from the sky, alighting gracefully upon her gloved wrist. Next to her, Tavish caught Thistle—and fed her the piece of meat.

Robina and Tavish's gazes met then and held—and warmth spread through Robina's belly. Something had shifted between them this morning. She wasn't sure what the change was exactly, only that she was starting to view Tavish Gunn, not as an oppressor or captor, but as someone she might come to like.

It was snowing again when Tavish stepped out into the bailey. The noon meal had come and gone, and afterward, Robina had gone upstairs to spend the afternoon making holly wreaths for Yule with her maid, Fiona.

Left to his own devices, Tavish went out to check on the horses. The Eve of Yuletide was just a day away now, and the weather seemed to have turned even colder. It was difficult to exercise the horses in deep snow—they would be restless.

But as Tavish approached the stables, shouting reached him.

He frowned. The commotion was drifting out from the stables.

Shouldering open the doors, he stepped into the wide aisle between the rows of stalls, the musty smell of horse greeting him. A wall of leather, fur, and plaid-clad bodies blocked his view, but it was evident from their excited voices that a brawl was going on.

Mouth thinning, Tavish elbowed his way through their midst. Grunts and curses followed, although his warriors stilled their complaints when they saw their clan-chief amongst them.

They pulled back, giving Tavish an uninterrupted view of the fight.

Tavish's jaw clenched when he spied Roy and Will slinging punches at each other. Their two other brothers, Blaine and Evan, stood at the side-lines bellowing encouragement, while the horses snorted nervously in their stalls.

Roy was far bigger and stronger than Will, who had a leaner, lankier build—and Roy was laying into his younger brother with such viciousness that Tavish's step faltered a moment.

"What's going on here?" he growled to Blaine.

Grinning, Blaine glanced his way. "Roy took offense to something Will said."

"Aye," Evan chipped in. "Will's smart mouth has gotten him a hiding this time."

Actually, the fight didn't look entirely one-sided. Blood trickled from Roy's nose, and he wore a twisted, mean look on his face that Tavish recognized well. Roy had the worst temper of any of them, one that was a match for their late father's.

And as Tavish moved forward to intercept them, Roy spat out a filthy insult and head-butted Will. His younger brother staggered back, but Roy didn't let up. Instead, he grabbed him by the hair and smashed him in the face with his fist before driving a knee into his belly.

"Roy!" Tavish snapped. "Stop this!" Roy ignored him. Will sank to his knees, and still gripping him by the hair, Roy smashed his head down on the cobbled floor.

Will's body went limp.

Letting go of Will's hair, Roy rose above him and started to kick his prone form.

Tavish sucked in a deep breath, his temper rising like a sudden draft of wind. "Roy," he barked. "Cease this!"

But Roy did not.

Tavish's blow caught him unawares. It was a hard hit to the side of the head, a 'haymaker', designed to topple Roy in one blow—and it did.

The big man fell sideways, collapsing against the frame of one of the stalls.

Meanwhile, Will lay face-down and worryingly still upon the cobbles.

Breathing hard, fury writhing in his gut, Tavish went to Will. Taking him by the shoulder, he rolled him over.

Blood trickled down his brother's brow from a gash upon his forehead. He was still breathing, yet he hadn't come to.

Tavish glanced up, his gaze spearing Roy. The warrior had sunk to his knees and was shaking his head, dazed.

Around them, the stable had gone deathly silent. Blaine and Evan were no longer grinning like fools. Both of them had been at the receiving end of Roy's temper in the past, yet it was entertaining to see someone else get pummeled by him.

However, Roy had taken it too far this time.

Will's face had drained of all color, and his breathing was erratic.

"Ye shouldn't have interfered, Tav," Roy mumbled, meeting Tavish's gaze as his vision cleared. "This was between me and Will."

Tavish held Roy's stare. There was no missing the challenge, the belligerence. This had to be nipped in the bud.

"I'll say this just once, Roy," he growled, his voice cutting through the now silent stable. "If I catch ye raising yer fists to anyone in this castle, *ever* again, ye shall be banished from it." Tavish paused there, letting his words sink in. Roy's gaze narrowed, his expression turning mean once more. "And if Will doesn't wake from the thrashing ye've just given him, I will personally flog ye before casting ye out."

9

RESTLESS

ROBINA RAISED A goblet to her lips and took a sip of wine. A fabulous spread of food lay before her, for it was the eve of Yule—and the cooks had put on a feast of roasted goose, stuffed with pork and chestnuts. Platters of braised kale, buttered carrots, and fresh bread accompanied the goose. Boughs of holy and ivy decorated the great hall, as did pretty wreaths on each table.

But the atmosphere at the table was anything but festive.

Tavish wore a hooded expression as he helped himself to some goose, ignoring the wintry stare Roy was giving him. Roy's nose was swollen and looked to be broken. Farther down the table, Blaine and Evan had wary gazes—while Will was pale, his face mottled with bruises.

The whole keep had heard of the fight between Roy and Will a day earlier. Indeed, Will had been carried, insensible, up to his bed-chamber and had only awoken that morning.

Roy had almost killed him, yet the man didn't look remotely sorry about it.

Instead, he watched Tavish as if he'd have liked to take his fists to him too.

Robina suppressed a shudder. Roy Gunn was more than a brute—he was trouble. She'd already warned Tavish about him, and the urge to repeat it bubbled up inside her.

But when she glanced her husband's way and saw the watchful set of his features, she realized the warning was unnecessary. After the incident in the stables, Tavish was keeping an eye on Roy.

He'd told Robina about the fight as they'd lain abed together in the darkness, explaining how Roy would have kicked Will to death if he hadn't interceded.

"Didn't anyone else try to stop him?" Robina had asked aghast.

"No," Tavish had responded, a note of bitterness lacing his voice. "Few do at Castle Gunn."

Tavish's words had haunted Robina ever since. What a harsh world she'd entered, one where brother was at odds with brother. She hadn't enjoyed the dynamic within her own family over the years, yet it now seemed idyllic compared to the relationship between the Gunn brothers.

"Is the feast to yer liking, Robina?"

Tavish's voice intruded then. Robina glanced up from where she'd been pushing her food around her platter before favoring him with a smile.

"Aye," she murmured.

Tavish's mouth quirked. "Roast goose doesn't grace our table very often ... my father only used to want it at Yule."

Robina held his gaze. "But ye are clan-chief now, Tavish ... ye can ask for it whenever ye wish."

His smile widened. "Aye ... ye are right."

Watching him, Robina realized that for all his calm aura of confidence, this role was still new to Tavish. It was no surprise the likes of Roy challenged him, for all of them were getting used to not having George Gunn at the helm.

Robina glanced away, spearing a piece of meat with her knife. "Yer father terrified me," she admitted.

Tavish huffed a wry laugh. "He scared all of us," he replied before leaning in close. "Even Roy minded his tongue around him."

Robina took a mouthful of goose—it really was delicious. Swallowing, she met her husband's eye once more. "George Gunn never had much time for women, did he?"

She wasn't sure why she asked him that, only that the more time she spent with Tavish Gunn, the more curious she grew about him and his upbringing.

Tavish inclined his head. "Ye are an observant one, Robina ... no ... except for the servants who warmed his bed ... he had little time for yer sex." Tavish paused then, swirling the wine in his goblet. "I doubt he cared much for our mother ... I don't think I ever heard him refer to her with affection ... either before or after her death."

Readying herself for bed behind the screen in the clan-chief's bed-chamber, Robina tried to quell the nervous fluttering in her belly.

Tavish had honored his word—the night before, he hadn't touched her or made any advances—yet all of this was so new to her.

It felt strange to share her bed with a man.

Leaving off the heavy robe—for it had gotten too hot and restrictive wearing it over the past couple of nights, Robina decided that she would go to bed clad in her night-rail. Although filmy, the garment covered her from neck to ankle.

Robina emerged from behind the screen, padding across to the bed, where Tavish waited. The glowing hearth across the room threw out a warm, golden light, and a candle flickered on the table next to the bed, illuminating the proud lines of her husband's face.

Slipping into bed, Robina pulled the covers up under her chin. Outdoors, the wind rattled the shutters and whistled against the walls.

"I wouldn't be surprised if another blizzard hits us tonight," Tavish said, breaking the ponderous silence between them. Robina wondered if he found this situation as awkward as she did. "We'll be snowed in by the Epiphany if it keeps up."

Robina pulled a face. "I was hoping to go hawking before then."

"And we will," Tavish assured her. The bed shifted, and she felt his gaze upon her. "I'm looking forward to it, Robina."

She looked at him then, steeling herself for the impact of their gazes meeting. She had to admit that her husband looked handsome lying there, his dark, unbound hair rippling across the pillow. His eyes were slate grey in the candlelight.

Their stare drew out, and Robina swallowed. Then, dragging up her courage, she spoke. "Fiona assures me that it only hurts a little ... the first time ... coupling ... I mean." She broke off there, mortification washing over her in a hot tide. Mother Mary, she hadn't meant to speak so frankly. She'd been mulling over Fiona's words for the last couple of days, and after her discussion with her husband on the roof, her mind would not let the subject go.

A slow smile crept over Tavish's face. "Fiona, eh? So it's true that she and Malcolm have been meeting ... I thought he was looking pleased with himself the other day."

Alarm flared within Robina. "Don't say anything ... please. I don't want to get them in trouble."

Tavish's smile faded. "I have no intention of speaking a word to either of them ... their business is their own." He paused then, his gaze ensnaring hers. "But Fiona likely speaks true." His gaze twinkled then. "Although, since I'm a man, I'm not the one to seek assurances from."

"Fiona gave me the impression that coupling is … agreeable."

"*Agreeable?*" He propped himself up onto an elbow and raised an eyebrow. Amusement gleamed in his eyes. "That's an interesting way of describing it."

"She also said it's rumored ye know how to bed a woman."

Hades, what was wrong with her mouth tonight? It seemed to have a will of its own. She'd only imbibed one goblet of wine with her meal, yet she felt strangely bold as she lay talking to her husband.

To her surprise, Tavish laughed, the warm sound filtering over the chamber. "Did she? What else did saucy Fiona tell ye?"

"Just that." Robina glanced away, sure that her face would now be as red as a holly berry.

"Well, I'm flattered that word of my prowess circulates the castle," he replied, mirth in his voice. "Although, since I've only ever bedded two women within these walls, it's likely unfounded."

Robina couldn't help it; curiosity got the best of her, and she looked at him once more.

A smile curved Tavish's mouth, and he was looking at her in a way that made Robina feel all hot and restless.

"They were both servants?" she asked.

He nodded.

Robina wanted to ask more, yet this time good sense checked her. If she was truthful, she probably didn't need to know about Tavish's past conquests.

Silence fell between them once more, and the unsettling restlessness within Robina grew. "I'm not as scared as I was," she admitted quietly, "about what happens between husband and wife."

His gaze turned limpid. "If ye like, I can show ye a little of how yer body can respond to a man's touch," he replied, his voice a low, sensual rumble. "Nothing more than that … I promise."

Robina's breathing quickened, heat pooling in her lower belly. "I'd like to touch ye instead," she whispered. "Will ye let me … will ye show me what to do?"

Tavish stared at her a moment, his eyes growing dark. "Aye," he replied, a slightly strangled edge to his voice. "Are ye sure that ye are ready?"

"As long as we end things there, aye."

Robina's heart was now beating wildly. For some reason, the thought of touching him was less frightening than the other way around. This way, she could control the encounter.

"Very well." Tavish rolled onto his back. "Go ahead, wife."

There was no mistaking the challenge in his voice. "When it gets to the critical point, I shall guide ye."

Her mouth dry with both excitement and trepidation, Robina sat up and rolled down the coverlet, revealing her husband's naked torso. He wore woolen leggings to bed tonight, although there was no mistaking the arousal that tented them.

Robina's pulse started pounding in her ears.

She couldn't believe she was looking upon her husband in this way. However, she'd thought much about the things her mother and nurse had brought her up to believe. She didn't want to be kept prisoner by them any longer.

Cool air feathered across the bed now that she'd drawn back the covers, yet neither Robina nor Tavish paid the chill any mind. He was staring up at her, while she slowly reached out, running her fingertips from the hollow of his throat and down across the sculpted planes of his chest.

He shivered under her gentle touch, and she noted that his nipples had hardened into tight buds. Following instinct, she bent down and brushed her lips across them.

Tavish uttered a soft groan. His arms lay by his sides, and she noted his hands flexed—yet he didn't reach for her. She was grateful. She wanted to be able to touch him uninterrupted, to explore his body without distraction or fear.

The long, lean length of his torso, the way his belly hollowed, and the way the dark hair on his chest arrowed down to the waistband of his leggings made her breathing come in soft pants.

Tavish Gunn was a delight to look upon, she realized.

Leaning down once more, she trailed her lips over his chest, breathing in the warm musk of his skin, and down his belly. Her hair, unbound and brushed out, trailed after her, shielding her face from him.

Robina reached the waistband of his leggings and straightened up. The tenting of the material was even more evident than before.

"Ye can touch me there, Robina." Tavish's voice was husky, imploring. "If ye wish."

Did she?

Robina swallowed. Aye, she did. Curiosity and something else—a sensation that made her feel breathless and needy, writhed within her.

With a trembling hand, she reached out, trailing a fingertip down the long hard length of his outlined erection, from tip to root.

10

IN HAND

TAVISH FOUGHT THE urge to reach for her, to pull her down into his arms and claim her mouth with his.

Did Robina have any idea what she was doing to him?

With just one touch, she'd made his rod ache with need. And now, sitting back on her heels, she was gazing down at the bulge in his leggings with an expression of rapt fascination.

Lord, if she continued staring at his groin like that, he'd spill.

His breathing caught then, as she reached out once more, trailing her fingertip down the length of his engorged shaft.

"It's so hard," she whispered.

"Aye," his voice was choked now. "See what effect ye have on me, Robina?"

She glanced up, her hazel eyes widening as her gaze met his. Her throat bobbed as if fear warred with desire.

Moments passed, and then she looked away, gazing down at his groin once more. She stroked him again, more firmly this time—and then, drawing in a shaky breath, she took hold of the waistband of his leggings and rolled them down over his hips.

Tavish's rod sprang up to meet her, swollen and ready.

Robina stilled, her gaze wide as she stared at it.

Tavish couldn't take his eyes off her face. Her expression was a picture: a blend of delight, shock, and nervousness. A faint blush now stained her cheekbones.

Tavish's fingernails dug into his palms as he clenched his hands tighter.

It was killing him not to reach for her.

Robina reached out once more then, stroking the length of him again before cupping his bollocks.

Tavish groaned.

"What do I do next?" she murmured, her voice delightfully breathy.

"Take me in hand," Tavish replied, a rasp to his voice now. "Here …" He uncurled his fists and reached up, taking her hand and folding her fingers around the base of his rod. "Aye … firmly … like that." Christ's bones, he was going to explode. The feel of her cool, slender fingers gripping him was nearly too much.

"Aye … and what now?" she whispered.

"Ye stroke me … like this." His hand remained on hers as he guided it up to the swollen head of his shaft and then down.

Tavish let go of her hand then, fisting his own by his side once more as Robina started to work him.

Her attention was wholly upon her task, her chest rapidly rising and falling now. She wore a flimsy night-rail, and the firelight illuminated the jutting lines of her small, high breasts, the nipples hard and dark against the pale fabric.

Tavish's stomach muscles tightened as he imagined sucking them. He gritted his teeth. This was torture—pleasurable, yet barely endurable all the same.

"Harder," he grunted, angling up his hips to meet her. "Ye can tighten yer grip."

Robina's lips parted, and she nodded. She did as bid, pumping him more enthusiastically. And then, to his surprise, she halted, lowered her head, and kissed the glistening crown of his shaft.

Tavish's ragged breathing filled the bed-chamber. He whispered an oath then, a deep groan escaping when her pink tongue darted out, exploring him.

Pleasure barreled through Tavish in a hot tide. Lord, he was close to spilling now.

Robina drew back once more then, her hand working him, hard, as he'd asked for. He had no need to tutor her any further. This woman knew how to pleasure him.

Arching his hips off the bed, Tavish threw his head back, his climax hitting him with the full force of a battering ram. But Robina continued to stroke him, extending the pleasure that pulsed through his loins. Breathing hard, he glanced down and saw that he'd spilled his seed all over his belly.

Tavish's gaze shifted up to Robina's flushed face to see that her eyes still lingered on his groin in fascination.

A moment later, she looked up, their gazes meeting. And then, Robina favored him with a slow, delightful smile.

A grin stretched Robina's face as she urged her garron on, up the hillside. The pony's feathered fetlocks sank into the snow, although the morning was clear—the sun a hard white pinprick in a washed-out blue sky.

There had been a light dusting of snow overnight but not the blizzard that Tavish had been concerned about. As such, he'd suggested they go hunting after breaking their fast.

It was the day of Yule, and the servants were preparing a great banquet—one that would be even more elaborate than the evening before—to celebrate.

It was a treat indeed, to go hawking on Yuletide morning.

Reaching the crest of the hill, gloved arm held aloft, with Moth perched there, Robina glanced over her shoulder at the man who'd followed her up the hill. Like her, the Gunn clan-chief rode a hardy highland pony—a good choice when crossing snowy terrain. These garrons were as surefooted as mountain goats.

Robina's excited grin softened to a smile as her gaze lingered on her husband. A heavy fur about his shoulders and his sparrow hawk, Reaper, perched upon his outstretched wrist, Tavish Gunn definitely drew the eye. He'd tied back his long dark hair at the nape this morning, yet Robina could still remember it, fanned out around his head upon the pillows as his eyelids flickered closed, his face contorting in pleasure.

To her surprise, she'd enjoyed every moment of that encounter—even more so, for he'd let her take the lead, let her bring him to climax without reaching for her.

The whole scene had been incredibly exciting, and heat pooled in the cradle of Robina's hips as she recalled the details.

But best of all, after she'd retrieved a cloth and wiped Tavish's seed off his belly, they'd pulled up the covers—shutting out the night's bitter chill—and cuddled close.

Lying there, spooned by her husband's warm body as his breathing deepened and sleep took him, a feeling of contentment, unlike any Robina had ever known, had stolen over her.

If that was a taste of what it could be like between a man and a woman, did she need to be so afraid?

Robina glanced away from her husband then, urging her pony on once more, down the hill into the wide glen below. Her smile faded as she recalled all the frightening things her mother and Murdina had said over the years—the fear they'd both cultivated in her.

She was beginning to see that it had been, indeed, all a lie.

Pondering this, even as anger tightened her belly, Robina rode down into the glen and drew up her pony, waiting till Tavish stopped alongside.

"This spot will do nicely," he announced.

Robina smiled, her brooding forgotten. Indeed, the glen was a perfect hunting ground for the hawks. The birds would be able to spot prey easily against the pristine snow, and Robina and Tavish could view them hunt from this vantage point. "Aye," she murmured. "Let them stretch their wings."

With that, they removed the hoods from their hawks, loosed the jesses, and flung their arms skyward, letting the birds fly free.

Moth and Reaper needed no further encouragement. In an instant, the pair whirled high into the cloudless sky.

Robina watched them, her breath catching. It didn't matter how often she went hawking, she never tired of this sight.

"I like seeing ye smile, Robina." Tavish's voice intruded then. Tearing her gaze from the sky, she met her husband's eye. Tavish was looking at her with an intent expression that made a blend of excitement and nervousness flutter within her.

Swallowing, she held his gaze. "Thank ye for taking me out hawking," she murmured.

His cheek dimpled as his smile widened. "We shall do this regularly," he replied. "It is a passion we share ... and it gives us a chance to spend time together ... away from the prying eyes of servants and kin."

Robina cocked an eyebrow at this comment. It was true—there was little privacy in a stronghold, for a great number of people resided within. However, like her, Tavish had grown up inside the walls of a castle. She would have thought he was used to it.

"A clan-chief is always the center of attention," she replied after a pause. "I wouldn't think it would bother ye."

He huffed a laugh. "It doesn't ... usually." His gaze never wavered from hers. "But at times, it gets wearisome having four ruthless younger brothers ... all of whom covet my position."

"Surely, not *all* of them do?" She pointed out. "Just Roy?" Her brow furrowed as she said the name of the Gunn third-born. Just mentioning him cast a shadow over the morning. "Roy is more obvious than the others,"

Tavish replied, his features tightening, "but don't be fooled thinking Blaine, Evan, and Will aren't just as ambitious."

Silence fell between them then. Robina glanced up at where Moth glided overhead, surveying her domain. "Would Roy really have killed Will the other day?"

"Aye ... if I hadn't stopped him. He and Will have always clashed, although I've never known Roy to be so vicious."

She swung her attention back to Tavish, noting the veiled look in his eyes. This wasn't a subject he wanted to discuss, and yet she wanted to know more about the dynamics within the Gunn family. She was one of them now, and forewarned was forearmed. "Do ye know what set him off?"

Tavish met her eye before he shrugged. "Roy didn't say. But out of all of us, he takes after our old man the most." He paused then. "Our father once nearly beat Alexander to death, years ago now ... when Alex was around thirteen."

Robina's gaze widened, although she didn't reply, giving him the space to continue.

"It was over something inconsequential," Tavish said quietly, glancing away, his expression hooding. "Alex had merely answered him back over the noon meal. He lay unconscious for days after that beating." His gaze swung back to Robina then, spearing her. "Is it any wonder that we all grew up to be brutes?"

Robina stilled, taking in his proud profile. "Ye aren't a brute, Tavish," she murmured after a pause. "And *ye* choose whether or not to follow in yer father's footsteps."

11

UNDER THE MISTLETOE

ROBINA BREATHED IN the scent of pine and wood smoke, warmth flooding through her chilled limbs. She and Tavish had returned to the castle just in time for the Yule banquet. Stepping inside the great hall of Castle Gunn was a pleasant surprise. The servants had done a bonny job of decorating it for the evening before, yet today they'd added extra touches.

Boughs of drualus—mistletoe—trailed from the rafters, as did garlands of wreathed holly and pine. Banks of candles flickered in every corner, and a Yule log—a weighty branch of oak—smoldered in the hearth.

A woman sat at a harp near the fire, the lilting strains echoing above the rumble of conversation. Two Highland Collies, one of them Misty, sat at the harpist's feet.

Robina halted near the hearth, a smile curving her lips as she took a cup of mulled wine from a passing servant.

She did enjoy Yuletide, especially since it represented a turning point in winter's darkness—from this day on, they began the slow journey to spring.

"Ye know what happens to a woman who stands beneath a bough of drualus?" A rough male voice intruded then, interrupting Robina's reverie.

She glanced up to see Roy Gunn looming over her. His bruised and broken nose looked almost purple in the firelight, and although it had barely gone noon, his eyes were glazed with drink.

Glancing above her, Robina's chest constricted when she saw that, indeed, she'd stopped beneath a dangling sprig of mistletoe, the silver-green leaves and tiny white berries gleaming in the firelight.

Robina's jaw tensed. Of course she knew the tradition—nonetheless, it would be an icy day in hell before she'd let this man kiss her.

Stepping back, Robina tried to put some distance between them. However, with a grin, Roy reached out, gripped her by the arm, and hauled her toward him. Wine sloshed over the rim of her cup, staining the sleeve of the pine-green kirtle she'd worn for the Yule banquet. Roy paid it no mind.

His gaze was on her mouth. "Tradition is tradition ... sister-by-marriage. Let's taste those sweet lips."

"Kiss her, Roy, and I'll shove yer teeth down yer throat."

Roy's bulky shoulders stiffened, his gaze darting to where Tavish now stood.

Relief gusted from Robina at the sight of him. Tavish had been on the other side of the hall earlier talking to Blaine. But her husband must have spied Roy approaching her, for he had appeared at her side.

"Don't get yer braies in a knot, brother," Roy growled, his grip on Robina's arm tightening. "It's *tradition*."

Tavish's gaze narrowed, his face all taut angles. "Not anymore."

Long moments passed, and Robina was aware of conversation dying away around her. Even the harpist had stopped playing and was now gawking at them.

Robina's teeth clenched. Curse Roy—the man constantly stirred up trouble.

He now wore a truculent expression as he stared his elder brother down. But there was also a gleam in his eye. She realized then that his attempt at kissing her beneath the mistletoe was just a power play. He was seeking to undermine Tavish, to rile him.

She recalled the things her husband had revealed to her, earlier in the day, about how it was between the males of his family.

Her pulse began to race then. Roy would never stop challenging Tavish. He wanted to rule and could not bear to see another take the clan-chief's carven chair.

"Yer wife looks to be a cold bitch," Roy said finally, releasing Robina's arm with a sneer. "She's a fine match for ye, brother."

Tavish's dark brows crashed together. "Ye still haven't learned yer place, have ye?"

Roy's sneer morphed into a scowl. "No ... and I never will."

Rubbing her bruised arm, where Roy had so roughly gripped it, Robina eyed her husband and brother-by-marriage warily.

Hades, they weren't going to start brawling, were they? Not right before the Yule banquet?

Tavish set his cup of wine down on the mantelpiece before rolling up the sleeves of his quilted velvet gambeson. "I think it's time we clarified matters," he growled. "If ye want a hiding, ye shall have one."

"Tav." Will appeared then, stepping between his two elder brothers. The youngest of the Gunn brothers was still pale after the thrashing Roy had given him two days earlier, his face mottled with bruises. However, his gaze was determined as it met Tavish's. "The shitbag isn't worth the trouble ... not here ... not now." Will shifted his attention to Roy, whose lip had curled.

The loathing in Will's eyes chilled Robina.

Upon her arrival at Castle Gunn, she'd marked the simmering tension between the brothers. Of all of them, Tavish and Will appeared to get on the best. Perhaps, as the youngest brother, Will was less of a threat. Nonetheless, the exchanges she'd witnessed between Tavish and Roy always held an undertone of barely suppressed dislike, and ever since Tavish had broken up that fight, Roy's resentment had taken on a more menacing edge. Whether it happened today or not, blood would one day be spilled between the Gunn brothers—she knew it in her gut.

The silence drew out, and Robina readied herself for Tavish to throw the first punch. However, he surprised her by flashing Will a hard smile.

"Never were truer words said, Will." He then slapped his youngest brother on the back, even if tension vibrated off his lean form. Despite his words, he was only just holding himself in check. "Why give him what he wants?"

Exactly, Robina thought, noting the fury that contorted Roy's features. It was confirmation that he had, indeed, been deliberately goading Tavish.

Ignoring his brother, Tavish stepped close to Robina, flashed her a smile that didn't quite meet his eyes, and linked an arm through hers. "Come, mo chridhe, the Yule feast awaits."

The banquet passed without incident—mainly because Roy didn't join them.

After his near brawl with Tavish and ensuing humiliation, Roy had muttered a threat to Will and stalked from the hall.

His departure made relief sweep over Robina. As soon as Roy left, a festive mood returned to the hall. The harpist resumed playing, and the Gunns and their retainers took their seats at the long trestle tables that groaned under the weight of platters of roast meat—venison, mutton, and boar; bowls of buttered, mashed turnip; baskets of breads studded with walnuts; and platters of braised onions and kale. Servants had also carried in huge rounds of aged cheese as well as oatcakes drenched in honey.

Robina had rarely eaten so well—the cooks at Castle Gunn definitely had more talent than those at Kellie Castle.

The banquet drew out, the afternoon sliding into dusk before a lively ceilidh began. Robina and Tavish joined the dancers, twirling around the floor as the music soared. And as she danced, Robina found it impossible not to smile.

Perhaps life at Castle Gunn wouldn't be the ordeal she'd anticipated. Perhaps she could actually be happy here?

The reveling drew out into the evening and continued long after dusk settled over the world. Yet, eventually, Tavish bid his kin and retainers a good eve and led his wife upstairs.

Robina was glad to retire for the eve. Her feet ached from all the dancing, and she felt sleepy after the rich food and wine.

However, the feel of her husband's strong hand clasping hers made her stomach flutter nervously. She wasn't completely at ease when they were alone. Tavish's presence, his masculinity, overwhelmed her senses.

After what they'd shared the night before—after what she'd done to him—she now felt a trifle embarrassed.

Stepping inside their bed-chamber, the door thudding shut behind them, Robina turned to her husband. Her lips parted as she readied herself to speak to him. Yet she noted he wasn't looking at her but at the sprig of drualus that dangled from a beam directly overhead.

His mouth quirked. "How did that get there?"

Heat flushed through Robina. No doubt he thought she had deliberately hung it, to claim a kiss from her husband.

But she hadn't. In fact, she'd been about to ask if he could merely hold her close again tonight. She wasn't sure she was ready to take things further—not quite yet.

"Fiona must have hung it," she replied weakly.

Tavish's smile widened, and the fluttering in Robina's belly increased. Lord, he had a smile that did strange things to her insides. "Clever lass," he murmured, his gaze spearing Robina's. "Does this mean I may give my wife a kiss?"

Robina stilled. Of course, when he asked so politely, it would seem churlish to refuse him.

Nervously, she cleared her throat. "Aye ... go on then."

He laughed. "Try to appear a little pleased by the request, Robina. I won't bite."

Robina's jaw clenched. She didn't appreciate being teased, especially when she was this tense.

Sensing her shift in mood, Tavish sobered. Moving close, he reached up and cupped her cheeks.

Robina's breathing caught. She knew what she'd done to him last night should have broken the barriers between them, yet there was something about the melding of two mouths that seemed even more intimate.

Tavish leaned in, and his lips brushed hers, once, twice.

It was pleasant. His lips were soft, and up close, she inhaled the spicy scent of his skin.

A moment later, he kissed her again, the pressure firmer—and then his tongue parted her lips.

Robina gasped out at the invasion, yet Tavish's hands remained upon her cheeks, his tongue sliding gently against hers.

And to her surprise, Robina realized she liked it—as she had the first time he'd kissed her, before she'd panicked. The heat of his mouth, the way his lips slanted across hers, and the wicked glide of his tongue made heat ignite in the pit of her belly.

Without even understanding her reaction, she swayed against Tavish, losing herself in his embrace.

12

MAKE ME YERS

TAVISH HELD HER gently, as if she were something precious, something that might shatter if he handled her too roughly.

And all the while, his mouth gently explored hers, his tongue sliding against Robina's, teasing and testing.

Robina slowly gave herself up to the kiss, leaning into him further as his hands slid around to cradle the back of her head. He deepened the kiss then, his teeth grazing her lower lip.

Need arched up within Robina, and suddenly, she was kissing him back. Her hands went up, her palms splaying across the velvet material of his gambeson. She could feel the hardness of his chest, the warmth of his body beneath the quilted material.

Her palms itched to touch his naked skin.

"Robina," he whispered as he tore his lips from hers and let his mouth trail down her jaw to the column of her neck. There was a plea to his tone, a hoarseness to his whisper that made desire shiver through her.

Robina reached up, clinging to his shoulders as his lips explored the length of her neck before traveling up to the shell of her ear.

She trembled against him, her knees weakening.

Tavish claimed her mouth with his once again then, and this time, his kiss wasn't gentle. Instead, there was an urgency, a hunger, to it that made Robina respond in kind.

She kissed him wildly, forgetting how afraid she'd once been of him, forgetting all the terrifying things her mother and nurse had told her about what passed between a man and a woman.

How could something that felt so good, that made her body quiver with want, bring her harm?

The kiss continued, and Robina found herself leaning up against the wall, the length of her body pressed flush against Tavish's lean frame.

And then she felt the rock-hard column of his erection pressed against her belly.

Had she not already explored him the night before, had she not already taken him in hand and brought him to climax and watched his body respond to her touch, she might have been alarmed by the discovery.

But instead, a wild sensation—reckless and insatiable—reared up within her.

Without thinking, she pushed her hips against him, grinding slowly against his arousal.

The groan that rose in Tavish's throat inflamed her—and when he reached up and unbound her hair, letting it fall in waves over her shoulders, she undulated herself against him once more.

Murmuring an oath, Tavish tore his mouth from hers. His face was all lean angles, his grey eyes almost black in the firelight as he stared down at her. He reached up then, his fingers tangling in her hair, his lips, swollen from their passionate kisses, parting. "I think we should stop there," he rasped, his chest rising and falling sharply, "for if we continue in this vein, I may forget myself."

Robina stared up at him. Likewise, she was out of breath, yet her body tingled and pulsed in the aftermath of their embrace, and a deep ache pulsed between her thighs.

It hit her then that she didn't want him to stop.

She wanted Tavish Gunn to forget himself—she wanted him to make her forget as well.

Reaching up, she took his hand and entwined her fingers with his.

"I'm ready, Tav," she whispered, her voice catching as nervousness swelled in her breast. Pushing the sensation aside, she plowed on. Aye, she was a little scared of what was to come—yet she trusted her husband. She wanted to be joined with him. "I want to lie with ye ... tonight."

Tavish stilled, his gaze hooding with desire as he continued to stare down at her. "Are ye certain about this, Robina?" he asked, his voice husky now. "Once things go past a certain point, we can't go back."

"Aye," she whispered. "Make me yers."

Tavish watched her for a moment longer, and then he stepped back, his gaze raking over the length of her body—the look was so hot, so carnal, that Robina shivered. With just one look, he'd stripped her naked.

He reached out and began to unlace the bodice of her kirtle. His movements were deft, yet Robina noted the slight tremble in his fingers.

The man was holding himself on a tight leash.

Breathless, Robina watched him finish unlacing her bodice—and then he reached down, gripped her kirtle and lèine with his fists, and drew the garments up over her head.

Naked except for her slippers, Robina stood before him. Despite the roaring fire a few feet away, drafts still found their way into the chamber. As such, goosebumps prickled Robina's skin and her nipples hardened.

Tavish's heated gaze swept over her. "Lovely," he murmured. "Ye are even bonnier than I imagined."

Robina gave a nervous laugh. "Ye have imagined this moment?"

His gaze hooded further. "Many ... many times."

The sensual rumble of his voice made her shiver—and it had nothing to do with the chill drafts that pushed their way into the chamber through the gaps in the shutters.

It was in anticipation of what was to come.

Wordlessly, Tavish stripped off his own clothing, leather and velvet pooling around his feet.

Robina hungrily took in the hard, lean lines of his body and the magnificent shaft that bobbed before him. However, she didn't get the chance to gaze upon him for long before Tavish stepped close and lowered himself before her.

His hot mouth took a nipple and began to suckle her.

Robina's shocked gasp filled the chamber, and she clung to his shoulders once more, her eyes fluttering shut at the new, exciting sensation.

He drew the nipple deep into his mouth before gently pulling at it and grazing it with his teeth.

Robina gave a soft cry, arching against him as he focused his attention on her other breast.

She drew back slightly then, watching him in fascination. She'd always thought her breasts too small, yet they ached and throbbed under Tavish's touch; her nipples felt swollen and breathlessly sensitive.

A cry of disappointment ripped from her as he lowered himself further, his mouth leaving her breast and trailing down to her belly.

Yet the disappointment lasted only an instant, for when he nudged her thighs apart and lifted one of her legs over his shoulder, the feel of his finger sliding gently inside her made Robina gasp his name, her body trembling as he started to stroke her there. And then when he parted her wider still and she felt his mouth upon her, Robina unraveled.

Quivering, she arched her pelvis up to him, greedily taking the pleasure he gave her. She lost herself utterly in the sensation—all shyness, all nervousness and apprehension forgotten.

The feeling of his finger, sliding deep within her now and curling, as well as the flick and glide of his tongue, was too much.

With a raw cry, she arched against his mouth and shattered.

Tavish released her and rose to his feet then, sweeping Robina up into his arms. It was just as well since she had gone weak and boneless, aching pleasure still rippling through her loins.

Three paces took them to the bed, and Tavish lay her down upon it.

He then spread her wide once more and positioned himself between her thighs.

Fascinated, her breathing coming in needy pants, Robina watched him fist his quivering shaft and guide it into her.

"I will try to go slowly," he managed between gritted teeth, "yet this first time may hurt ye ... a little."

Aye, Fiona had warned her of that—although her mother had said much worse.

A flicker of apprehension surfaced then, as she recalled the chill that had slithered down her neck when Isla had told her that being taken by her husband the first time had made her feel as if she were being ripped asunder.

And yet, Tavish wouldn't cause her agony. She trusted him.

Inhaling deeply, she let her fears fall away and allowed her body to relax.

Tavish eased his way in, working his thick shaft into her tightness. Robina drew in deep, shuddering breaths, marveling at the fullness, at the feeling of being stretched.

There was a sting then, as he pushed past the barrier of her maidenhead, and she gasped, yet the discomfort was fleeting.

An instant later, he slid to the root, and the sensation of being completely filled made Robina catch her breath.

Tavish stared down at her, his face taut. "Are ye comfortable, lass?" he ground out.

"Aye," she breathed, tentatively rolling her hips and then gasping as pleasure rippled through her lower belly. "Oh ... aye!"

He muttered a curse then, his fingers digging into her hips. She watched him withdraw, with aching slowness, before sliding deep once more. The look on her husband's face was so strained, he almost looked as if he were in pain.

He repeated the act—another long, slow stroke that made Robina whimper in pleasure—and she realized he was holding himself back, for her.

Wrapping her legs around his hips, she drew him against her, angling herself to meet his next stroke.

"More," she gasped. "Harder."

"Robina, I—"

"Harder!"

With a strangled sound, he held himself up over her and started to pound into her in deep, hard thrusts.

Aching heat surged in the cradle of Robina's hips, her cries echoing through the chamber.

The wet sound of their bodies coming together was so erotic that she writhed against him, demanding more, crying his name again and again. Tavish let himself go, his own cries joining hers until he found his release inside her, a violent shout tearing from his throat.

Tavish collapsed on top of his wife. His breath came in ragged gasps, sweat bathed his skin, and his limbs shook.

He'd never climaxed like that before, so hard that his vision had actually darkened for a few moments.

Aware that he was likely crushing his slender wife, Tavish rolled off her onto his back. There he lay, one arm thrown over his eyes, as he struggled to regain his breath. He felt strange in the aftermath of the passionate coupling—his chest ached, and his throat was tight.

"Tavish?" A soft voice reached him, and he removed his arm from across his eyes to see that Robina was staring down at him.

Christ's bones, she was a sight. Her long dark hair fell around her shoulders in wild disarray; her cheeks, neck, and breasts were flushed; her hazel eyes were bright; and her lips were bee-stung from his kisses.

"Are ye well?" she asked huskily, reaching out and placing a soft hand on his chest where his heart still bucked against his ribs.

Tavish stared up at her. "Not really," he admitted, a trifle shakily. Hades, what was wrong with him?

13

ALL OF YE

ROBINA'S HAZEL EYES widened, and Tavish saw worry shadow them.

He reached up, his hand covering hers that still lay upon his chest, and squeezed gently. "I wanted to go gently with ye, but I lost control, lass … did I hurt ye?"

She shook her head.

Tavish's chest constricted. "Are ye certain?"

"Ye didn't hurt me," she whispered, her gaze gleaming now. "I wanted it, Tav … I wanted ye to give me all of ye."

He stared up at her, the ache in his chest increasing. He wasn't sure he liked the sensation—he'd never felt like this after taking a woman.

Exposed. Raw. Vulnerable.

"It's never been like that for me," he admitted huskily after a pause. It was true—he'd always held a piece of himself back with his lovers. And now, in the aftermath of this passionate coupling with Robina, he understood why.

This woman had stripped away his shields, his armor. He felt as if he was revealing his soft underbelly to her—and he was, both literally and figuratively.

Tavish didn't like feeling so exposed.

Letting his guard down wasn't wise. He lived in a den of wolves, and although Robina was supposed to be his safe haven—one he'd longed for—the reality of what he felt for this woman scared him. He hadn't been prepared for the emotional intensity that had come with their joining.

Holding his gaze, Robina favored him with a tremulous smile. "Is it not always like that then?" she asked, shyly. "Between husband and wife?"

"I don't know," he replied, deciding it was best to be honest with her. "But ye are quite a woman."

It was the truth. He'd imagined their first coupling numerous times but hadn't anticipated just how lusty his wife was under her nervous, reticent façade. Her passion delighted him, however, the churning melee within him did not.

"Come here, wife," he murmured, pulling her against his chest.

She curled into him, warm and soft, her breath feathering against his neck, and something raw tugged deep inside Tavish's chest. He felt torn between wanting to protect this lovely, vulnerable woman who had just given herself to him and shielding his own heart.

Robina awoke to find Tavish gone. Stretching in the big bed, she reached out to where her husband had lain. The mattress was still warm. He hadn't been gone long.

A sigh of contentment mixed with longing rose up within her. She'd just passed the most magical, and most revealing, night of her life.

She knew now that her mother and Murdina had filled her ears with lies, with poison, all those years.

Coupling didn't bring agony and humiliation—not with the right partner.

Tavish had shown her another world.

She'd hoped he would take her again, yet he'd pulled her close, and they'd fallen asleep like that, wrapped in each other's arms.

Tavish had seemed a little odd in the aftermath of their coupling as if he was struggling with something.

Robina understood how he felt—for she hadn't expected that either. However, he'd appeared disturbed by it.

Pondering this, Robina swung her legs over the edge of the bed and got up.

It was early; the faint watery light of dawn was just starting to filter through the shutters.

Shivering, Robina added another lump of peat to the guttering hearth and then dressed. It was a chill morning, and so she chose her warmest woolen kirtle and wrapped a fur shawl around her shoulders.

Impatient to seek out her husband, she pulled on a pair of fur-lined boots and went next door to the solar. She'd expected to see him there, warming his hands before the fire, but the large chamber was empty.

The door opened then, and Fiona entered, bearing a tray of bannocks, butter, and honey.

"Good morning, my lady," the lass chimed with an impish smile. "Did ye sleep well?"

Robina's cheeks warmed. Of course, she and Tavish had made quite a bit of noise the night before. Did half the keep now know the laird and his wife had enjoyed a night of passion?

"Aye, thank ye," Robina replied, deciding it was best to brazen the moment out.

Fiona's smile widened. "I'm pleased to hear it." The warmth in her maid's voice eased Robina's embarrassment. Fiona wasn't like her mother—she was genuinely happy that Robina and Tavish were forming an attachment to each other.

"Have ye seen the laird?" Robina asked as she helped herself to a wedge of bannock, slathering it with butter and honey. She usually had a poor appetite in the morning—but not so today. "Has he gone up to the mews?"

Tavish had told her once that he often went up to the roof to watch the sun rise over the sea, or when he wanted some solitude. After his odd mood following their coupling, she wondered if he'd indeed gone there this morning.

Misgiving feathered through her then, puncturing the cloud of well-being that she'd been floating on since the night before. Something was amiss.

"No, my lady," Fiona replied as she went to tend to the fire. "I saw him heading toward the stables with two of his brothers."

A short while later, after finishing a wedge of bannock and washing it down with a cup of milk, Robina emerged from the keep into the snow-covered bailey.

More snow had fallen overnight, and a crisp crust crunched underfoot as she drew her shawl close and made her way across to the stables.

The chill bit into the exposed skin of her face and hands and drilled through her layers of clothing. The dawn of Saint Stephen's—the day after Yule—was a cold one indeed.

It was a still morning, yet to the east, the sky glowed a silver pink. A snow-sky if Robina had ever seen one.

She was surprised then when she saw Tavish lead a saddled horse out of the stables, excited dogs capering at his heel. Two more men—Evan and Will Gunn—followed close behind. All three brothers carried longbows and quivers of arrows slung over their backs.

"A cold morning for a ride," Robina greeted Tavish, approaching him. Meeting her eye, Tavish favored her with a devil-may-care smile.

"Aye, wife, ... but we Gunns don't feel the cold."

"It's our Saint Stephen's hunt." Will piped up with a grin. "A Gunn tradition."

Robina nodded, even if a pang constricted her chest. Tavish knew she loved to hawk and hunt and would have gladly accompanied them.

However, clearly, she wasn't invited this morning.

She stood there, drawing her shawl closer still, and wondered if her husband would bestow her with a kiss before heading out.

Yet Tavish didn't.

Instead, he checked his horse's girth and swung up onto the saddle before turning to the men at the gates and calling out, "Raise the portcullis."

Tavish then turned back to Robina and favored her with another smile—the expression held the arrogance that had once galled her about the Gunn males. But now, since she'd gotten to know her husband, and since they had become intimate, she found his arrogance oddly alluring.

Goose, she chided herself. *I do believe ye are smitten.*

Nonetheless, this arrogant and slightly aloof clan-chief hardly seemed the same man who'd given himself to her the night before.

Seated atop his shaggy, feather-footed mount, he seemed untouchable—unreachable.

"I shall see ye at noon, wife," he said then before whistling to his dogs and reining his horse around.

Robina watched as the party thundered out of the bailey and onto the wooden bridge beyond. She stood there for a few moments after their departure, as snow started to fall silently from the dusky sky—and the same misgiving she'd felt earlier in the bed-chamber returned.

However, this time the sensation was sharper and accompanied by a knot in her belly.

Was Tavish Gunn one of those men she'd heard the servants at Kellie Castle gossip about? The kind to lose interest in a woman once a conquest had been made?

The memory of Robina's lovely face, her cheeks flushed with cold, lingered in Tavish's mind as he led his brothers across the western hills.

She'd looked achingly beautiful, standing there, her face framed with fur. He'd wanted to step forward, to haul her into his arms for a searing kiss—despite any jeers and taunts from his brothers.

But he hadn't.

Instead, he'd favored his wife with a careless farewell as if she hardly mattered to him. He'd seen the hurt in her eyes—for he knew Robina liked to hunt. And yet he'd deliberately not invited her.

He needed some time apart from his alluring wife. Time to clear his head.

That morning, he'd awoken before dawn, rolled over, and gazed down at Robina's sleeping face. Terror had swept over him—a chill, prickling sensation that had cramped his gut and catapulted him from the bed.

This was what he'd wanted, wasn't it? He'd lusted after Robina Oliphant, had dreamed of making her his for years—but now that she'd given herself to him, the reality of what it meant to be truly close to another person hit him like a mallet between the eyes.

Tavish had never trusted anyone, never been truly open with anyone—and to let his guard down now went against every survival instinct he had.

Snow fluttered into Tavish's eyes, and he brushed it aside, his gaze sweeping the snowy vista before him. Woodland lay farther west, and in it roamed a herd of red deer. Their tracks would be easy to find and follow in the snow.

"Come on!" he shouted to his brothers, who were lagging behind. Enough fawning over his wife. A clan-chief needed to remain tough, aloof. "Race ye both to the woods."

14

WRESTLING IN THE SNOW

THE BROTHERS RETURNED to Castle Gunn with a dead hind slung over the back of Evan's horse. The snow fell heavily now, the thick flakes settling upon the backs of the hounds and frosting the manes and forelocks of the horses. They'd been fortunate, for although the snow had continued to fall throughout their hunting trip, the weather hadn't worsened further.

As the bulk of the fortress appeared in the distance, through the swirling snow, Will cut Tavish a look. There was a shrewd glint in his eye that Tavish didn't miss.

"What?" Tavish frowned. He'd caught the youngest of his brothers favoring him with veiled glances all morning—it was starting to get on his nerves.

"Things seem to have thawed between ye and yer bride," Will observed. This comment brought a snigger from Evan.

Tavish ignored the references to the noises they'd all likely heard the night before.

Indeed, Tavish had forgotten himself. He'd forgotten that, despite the thick stone walls, sound carried at Castle Gunn. He'd been so lost in his wife, he hadn't cared.

However, his brothers' jibes in the aftermath were wearing.

"I would have thought ye would have lingered in yer bed this morning," Will continued, undaunted by the clan-chief's silence. "Not drag yer carcass out to join us."

"Aye," Evan grunted. "Blaine and Roy couldn't be bothered … and we didn't expect to see ye either."

Tavish flashed them a wolfish smile. "What … and break with tradition?"

Will snorted. "None of us have a comely wife warming our bed." He cut Tavish another sly look. "Unless yer insistence on keeping with tradition has more to do with keeping Robina in her place." He paused then. "Perhaps ye are more like our father than ye realize?"

A shiver that had nothing to do with the snow, or the biting north wind, cut through Tavish.

Will's words hadn't been meant as a compliment.

All of George Gunn's sons had obeyed him, minded him, yet it hadn't been out of respect but fear. Their father had ignored the woman who'd borne him five sons and hadn't grieved her passing.

He'd been a selfish, cold man who'd taken his pick from the prettiest servants.

Over the years, Tavish had often seen the cowed, haunted look in the serving lasses' eyes the morning after they'd shared the clan-chief's bed. George Gunn had been a brute—and he'd tried to beat and bully his sons into his own image.

The likes of Roy needed no tutoring, yet it galled Tavish to have Will make a comparison between them.

I'm not like that bastard, he thought, clenching his jaw.

But as the dark walls of Castle Gunn loomed above them, Tavish wondered if, indeed, there was no escaping the fact that George Gunn's blood flowed through his veins.

Roy and Blaine were overseeing a wrestling match in the bailey when Tavish, Will, and Evan rode under the portcullis.

Seemingly oblivious to the swirling snow, two warriors, stripped to the waist, their bare feet reddened with cold, held each other in a death grip.

Around them, the other men heckled and shouted while they exchanged bets.

The noise of their cheering echoed off the stone walls of the fortress and made the horses snort and side-step nervously.

Blaine called out to his brothers, who acknowledged him with a nod, yet Roy ignored them.

Instead, he heckled one of the wrestlers, who'd just slipped in the snow. "Useless shitbag!" he roared. He then ripped off his cloak and lèine, heeled off his boots, and shoved the losing opponent aside. "Let me show ye how it's done."

Behind Tavish, Will muttered something under his breath. Tavish's mouth thinned. These days, he shared Will's deep dislike for Roy. The meanness and spite their brother carried was bone-deep these days. Like Will's, Roy's face still bore the bruises and swellings from the other day, yet—as always—Roy Gunn was spoiling for a fight.

A roar went up as Roy felled his opponent and then ground him face down into the snow with an elbow between the shoulder blades.

Roy's gaze then cut across the bailey, to where Tavish and the others had just dismounted. There was no mistaking the challenge in his voice as he called out. "Yer turn, Tav … let's see how long ye last against me!"

The roar of men's voices drew Robina and many others out of the keep.

"They're wrestling in the snow, Lady Robina," Fiona informed her, her voice tight with excitement as they cast fur mantles about their shoulders and followed the servants outside. "Malcolm says the laird and Roy Gunn have already gone five rounds!"

Robina's belly tightened at this news before her jaw tensed. *Men.* Why did they always have to be so aggressive with each other? Her own brothers had scrapped constantly over the years. However, here at Castle Gunn, the sparring had an edge of danger to it.

Roy didn't bother to hide his hatred for Tavish—and never missed an opportunity to undermine him. Had Tavish just played straight into his hands?

A crowd had gathered in the heart of the bailey, although the servants parted respectfully to let Lady Gunn and her maid into their midst.

An icy wind whipped across the keep then, chapping Robina's cheeks.

Hauling her mantle tightly around her, she let her gaze settle upon the two half-naked men who grappled with each other. Tavish and Roy didn't appear to notice the numbing cold.

Robina's breathing stilled as she watched them. It was hard to believe the pair were brothers, as, despite their dark hair and grey eyes, Tavish and Roy Gunn looked nothing alike. Tavish was long and lean while Roy was built like an ox—the latter's huge shoulders gleamed with sweat. The man was built for wrestling, as he could use his superior size and weight to his advantage.

However, his opponent moved with a litheness and agility that Roy lacked.

Tavish twisted like an eel under Roy's bruising grip, his bare toes digging into the snow as his brother tried to topple him.

Robina had stopped next to Will and Evan, who were looking on, their grey eyes gleaming.

"It's the deciding round," Will informed her with a grin.

"Aye ... Roy's in a rage about it too," Evan quipped. "He'd hoped to trounce Tavish by now."

Indeed, Roy's bruised face had gone bright red, his eyes narrow slits. Sweat poured off his heavy brow.

In contrast, Tavish's lean face was taut in concentration, his brows knitted together as he resisted yet another attempt from Roy to topple him sideways.

Tavish struck then, his heel slamming down on Roy's foot before he wrapped a leg around his brother's.

With a roar of rage, Roy collapsed on his side.

Cheering erupted from the sidelines.

Robina, who had been as tense as a drawn bow-string during the bout, let out the breath she hadn't realized she'd been holding.

"We have a winner!" Blaine called out. "Our clan-chief is the victor!"

More cheering ensued, and glancing around at the faces of the onlookers, Robina noted the genuine joy on their faces.

They respected Tavish, she realized. They wanted him to best his thuggish brother.

But Roy wasn't taking his defeat well. His face had gone an ugly shade of purple as he staggered to his feet. He then growled a curse and spat on the snow.

"Sore loser!" Will crowed, his tone deliberately goading.

Tavish straightened up and reached for the lèine Evan passed him. However, his attention wasn't on Roy, his other brothers, or the applauding crowd, but upon Robina.

His gaze was searing.

Heat ignited in Robina's chest, sweeping over her as if she'd just sunk to her chin in a bathtub of steaming water.

It was an intimate look, one of sultry promise.

Tavish barely glanced in his brother's direction as Roy shouldered his way out of the crowd and stormed off. The clan-chief then shrugged on his lèine and flashed his wife a grin. The expression was cocky and purely masculine.

And in an instant, Robina forgot her hurt and burgeoning worries of that morning.

When he smiled at her like that, the rest of the world faded—under its force, she could barely recollect her own name.

Maybe she'd worried unnecessarily—things were new between them after all. A lifetime of feeling misunderstood had left Robina sensitive to any perceived slight.

But when he looked at her with such melting eyes and that sensual smile, she could almost believe she'd imagined he'd rejected her.

15

STRANGERS ONCE MORE

HOWEVER, ROBINA DIDN'T imagine things the following morning when her husband rolled away, gently disentangling his limbs from hers, and rose from the bed.

Robina awoke, blinking as her eyes adjusted to the darkness. It was early—before dawn—and too early to be rising from their bed.

Rubbing her eyes, she sat up. "Tavish," she murmured, her voice husky with sleep. "Where are ye going at this hour?"

"Go back to sleep, lass," Tavish replied, his voice a low rumble in the dim light. The fire in the hearth had dimmed overnight and was close to going out. A deep chill had fallen over the chamber.

Robina tensed, her gaze following his tall frame as he finished dressing and then crossed to the hearth. She couldn't believe he was leaving again. Moments later, crackling filled the chamber when he fed the fire and stirred the embers to life with a poker.

"Before we coupled for the first time, ye always lay abed with me in the morning," she said softly, "but now ye sneak off like a thief."

Tavish snorted. "I'm not *sneaking off*."

"Then why won't ye come back to bed?"

"I'm an early riser."

"An early riser?" She couldn't help it; her voice rose a notch. "But it's the middle of the night."

He snorted again, turning to her. Ruddy firelight caressed his hawkish features, yet Robina could see irritation there.

Her belly tightened.

He hadn't been irritated yesterday when he'd swept her off her feet and carried her to bed, kicking the chamber door closed behind him.

Tavish had then torn off her clothes and spread her out on the bed, taking his fill of her till they were both dripping with sweat and gasping for breath.

They'd spoken little in the aftermath of their coupling, and Robina had missed the easy conversation they'd shared following their wedding.

Now they'd become intimate, her husband didn't seem to want to talk to her anymore.

"Go back to sleep," he replied, his tone firm now. "I'll see ye later."

Robina stared up at him, hurt knotting in her chest. "I don't understand," she said, her voice barely above a whisper. "Why have ye changed?"

"I haven't changed, woman," he grumbled, his voice edged with irritation.

"Aye, ye have," she replied, dogged now. "It takes a lot for me to trust others, Tav ... but yer gentleness with me, the way ye listened to me ... made me believe that there was one person at least in this world whom I could confide in, could rely on." She broke off there, trying to ignore the way her throat constricted and the hot tears that prickled her eyelids. She didn't want to weep, not now. "But did I form the wrong impression of ye?" she asked finally. "Is that not who ye really are?"

Tavish stared at her for a long moment, and then his gaze hooded. "Ye wed a Gunn, Robina ... we aren't like the men of yer clan."

She swallowed a bitter laugh at that. Aye, she knew all about the Gunns—but she also knew that the men of her own family didn't treat their women like queens.

"That's just an excuse," she said, her voice catching. "Ye aren't like the others, Tav ... ye are different."

He cocked his head. "Am I?" His features hardened then. "The fact of the matter is that ye hardly know me at all ... I was raised to fight, to see everyone as an adversary. I don't think I can be anyone else."

Robina drew herself up, her temper quickening. "That's nonsense. Ye decide who ye are, not yer kin ... or yer dead father." She paused then, swinging her legs off the bed as she rose to face him. "Don't ye want us to be close ... to be friends as well as husband and wife?"

Tavish shook his head and took a step back toward the door. "No," he said softly. "I can't give ye any more than this, Robina."

With that, he turned and stalked from the bedchamber, the door thudding shut behind him.

Tavish climbed the stairs to the roof, letting himself out onto its flat surface.

It had snowed again during the night, and a glittering white crust frosted the tower top and the crenellations. The mews lay in darkness at this hour. Yet the torches on the ramparts below cast a pale gold light over the fortress.

The sky was still shadowed, although the eastern horizon, where the dark bulk of the sea met the sky, held a faint glow.

Dawn was approaching,

Drawing his fur cloak about him, Tavish stared out into the pre-dawn gloom.

What's wrong with ye, man?

He'd acted like a complete dolt back in that chamber—had been callous and cold. He now wished he could take those words back.

But it was too late; they were already out there.

The sight of Robina sitting naked on the bed when he'd turned from the fire, her dark hair spilling over her shoulders, her eyes soulful and trusting, had branded him.

She wanted to be close to him, to develop a bond between them, yet now that he'd won her, Tavish was paralyzed by fear.

Fear of being known, of giving someone a weapon to use against him.

He was a survivor—and had only lived this long in such a hostile environment through wiles and ruthless cunning.

Robina would turn him soft, would give the likes of Roy weapons to use against him.

I can't let that happen.

And yet the crushing pain that rose under his breastbone when he recalled the hurt on his wife's face made Tavish realize that he was fighting a losing battle.

The truth was that he was desperately in love with his wife, and he wouldn't be able to keep his distance from her forever.

Coldness stole over him then; it was freezing up here this morning. But his focus wasn't on the cold but on his wife.

It had taken a lot for him to penetrate Robina's reservations, to get her to trust him. She'd just admitted as much.

Like him, Robina was wary of revealing her heart to anyone.

Tavish shivered as the gelid morning air bit into his exposed skin. But still, he lingered upon the roof. This place had always been where he went when he needed to sort out his thoughts and make difficult decisions

Aye, Robina would soon raise her shields again, and they would be strangers once more.

Tavish Gunn had a choice to make.

"Have ye seen the clan-chief?" Roy Gunn's casual question to Malcolm, the austringer, caught Robina's attention.

She'd broken her fast alone in the solar, again, before venturing out into the bailey in search of her husband.

It seemed she wasn't the only one looking for him.

Roy and Malcolm were standing by the stone well to one side of the keep. Neither had seen Robina as she stood in the shadows.

Robina wasn't sure why exactly she was bothering to seek her husband, for Tavish's words before dawn still stung—yet something within her wouldn't let things lie.

She didn't want to withdraw, to become the Robina of old. Tavish had freed her from that prison. With him, she hadn't needed to hold back. But now he was the one retreating, and she wasn't sure what to do about it.

Hunting her husband down likely wasn't the answer, but she couldn't remain in the solar pretending to care about embroidery or weaving. Tavish had given her a glimpse of happiness, of what their future could look like, and she didn't want to let it go.

Even so, she stepped back farther into the shadows as Malcolm replied. "Aye, I just saw him. He's up on the tower top ... exercising Reaper."

Roy nodded, his expression strangely inscrutable.

Then, without another word, the warrior turned and walked off in the direction of the steps leading up into the keep.

Robina waited until he'd disappeared inside before she picked up her skirts and followed.

"Good morning, Lady Robina," Malcolm called out to her cheerily.

Robina favored the austringer with a smile and a wave yet didn't break her stride.

There was something about Roy's manner this morning—a quiet cunning, a determination in his eyes—that she didn't like.

A storm had been brewing between Tavish and his brother for a while now—since before she'd arrived at Castle Gunn, she wagered—and it was about to break.

16

THE BREAKING STORM

THE HIGHER ROBINA climbed, the harder her heart pounded. Not from exertion, as she was used to climbing stairs multiple times a day—both here and at Kellie Castle—but from a growing sense of dread.

The back of her neck prickled.

She could hear the scuff of Roy's boots on the landing above. She was gaining on him yet didn't want to alert him to her presence.

All she could think about was the expressionlessness of his face in the bailey below contrasting against the gleam of his grey eyes.

The man was up to something.

Robina sped up, taking the steps two at a time now—not an easy feat with skirts swishing around her legs.

Rounding a corner, she spied Roy's broad form up ahead.

He reached for the handle of a heavy oaken door, drawing his dirk from his hip as he did so.

A scream rose in Robina's throat at the sight of the long, thin blade glinting in the light of a nearby cresset.

Oblivious to her presence, Roy shoved the door open and took the final set of stairs to the roof. Robina raced up the icy steps behind him before barreling out onto the tower top.

As she feared, Tavish had his back to them.

He was standing at the western edge of the tower, face tilted up as he watched his sparrow hawk swoop high overhead.

Roy raised his dirk high, aiming for a spot between the shoulder blades, and lunged.

"Tavish!" The scream ripped from Robina's throat. "Move!"

And he did.

Although her husband's attention had been elsewhere, his senses were sharp, his reactions honed. He side-stepped and swung around, just as Roy collided with one of the merlons that ringed the tower top.

Roy's curse rang through the still morning air, while above, Reaper's cry echoed him.

A heartbeat later, Roy recovered and went for Tavish again, blade flashing.

There was no time for Tavish to draw his own dirk. Instead, he stepped close, under Roy's guard, and grabbed his brother's thick wrist. "It's come to this, has it?"

"Aye," Roy snarled back. "It's time for ye to die, brother ... time for me to take yer seat."

A few yards away, Robina halted, her heart in her throat. *That traitorous bastard!*

Roy lunged forward then and head-butted his elder brother. Tavish hadn't anticipated the move, and he reeled back, losing his hold on Roy's wrist.

Tavish stumbled and fell, rolling across the snowy surface of the tower. Roy went after him, his face savage, dirk swiping—but despite that he was at a disadvantage, Tavish evaded him, rolling lithely to his feet and bouncing back as his brother's blade flashed just inches from his exposed throat.

Roy lunged again, and Tavish dove under his guard once more, aiming a punch squarely in his brother's gut.

Roy's grunt split the freezing air, and he made a grab for Tavish's hair—however, his elder was faster.

His next punch landed in Roy's groin, bringing the bigger man to his knees.

The brothers were locked in a stranglehold then, a parody of the wrestling match of the day before.

Roy was livid, the veins on his forehead bulging as he angled his blade toward Tavish's throat.

But Tavish held his wrists once more—and although he lacked his brother's brute strength, the blade wasn't giving an inch.

Frozen to the spot, Robina frantically glanced around. She wanted to help her husband, yet there was nothing upon the tower top that she could wield as a weapon—no brick or iron bar she could lob at Roy's head.

Desperate, as the dirk-blade glinted in the pale winter sun, she reached down and, scooping up snow in her hands, formed a hard-packed ball. She then stepped forward and hurled it at Roy.

It caught him hard on the cheek, the impact making him lurch sideways, his murderous gaze snapping to her.

The distraction was all Tavish needed. He drove Roy's wrist down and punched him in the face, crushing his already broken nose.

Roy's roar followed.

Tavish kept moving. He slammed his brother sideways and smashed his head up against one of the merlons.

The sickening, hollow thud of the impact made Robina's jaw clench.

She wasn't surprised when Roy slumped, insensible, against the wall, his dirk slipping from his fingers.

Tavish grasped the weapon and tossed it in Robina's direction. Even though Roy was momentarily incapacitated, he wasn't taking any chances.

Expression stone-hewn, Tavish drew his own dirk then and stood over his brother, waiting for him to awaken. Meanwhile, Reaper swooped down and perched on one of the merlons. The sparrow hawk studied the brothers, his gaze dispassionate.

Wordlessly, Robina stepped forward and picked up the dirk from the snow. As she did so, she heard Roy groan.

His eyes flickered open, unfocused at first, before his gaze settled upon the clan-chief's face.

For a few moments, the two brothers merely looked at each other.

"There are some lines that can never be crossed, Roy," Tavish said, his voice low and cold. "I've warned ye what would happen if ye ever challenged me."

Roy stared up at him, loathing twisting his face. However, this time, he had nothing to say.

Roy Gunn was driven from the castle that morning.

It was a brutal scene, yet one that Robina forced herself to watch.

She'd thought her husband would flog Roy for attempting to murder him, yet instead, he let the inhabitants of the fortress deal out justice.

Dressed in nothing more than braies, boots, and a thin lèine, Roy stumbled across the bailey hounded by howling servants. They pelted him with anything to hand: rotten food, animal manure, and stones.

Their fury and venom was shocking to behold, revealing the depth of dislike the folk here had for Roy.

Blood trickled down his temple where a stone from one of the stable hands had caught him, and as a turnip smacked him across the back of the head, Roy tripped and sprawled headlong in the snow.

Robina glanced over at her husband and saw the severe lines that etched his face, the fury that simmered in his storm-grey eyes. His three other brothers—Will, Blaine, and Evan—all stood behind the clan-chief, their expressions similarly grim.

All of them continued to watch Roy, yet none of them moved to aid him.

"Ye are banished from Castle Gunn." Tavish's voice carried across the bailey as the clamor of the mob died down for an instant. "Ye are cast from this clan ... and if ye ever set foot on my lands again, I shall hang ye from the walls."

The threat hung coldly in the air, and Roy snarled, before one of the serving lasses—Jean, the young woman Robina had seen him harass—emptied a bucket of slops over his head.

The mob closed in then, and one of the men picked up a brick, advancing toward Roy.

Picking himself up, Roy lurched forward, fleeing the mob's wrath.

Watching the scene unfold, Robina suppressed a shudder. It was a frightening thing to behold—the fury of an enraged crowd—and she saw how Roy's expression altered when he glanced over his shoulder at the encircling mob.

There was fear in his eyes now.

He bolted for the gate, ducking his head as projectiles flew at him. An instant later, he disappeared under the portcullis and onto the bridge beyond.

His pursuers followed.

A heavy silence fell in the bailey then as the shouts and cries drew away.

Eventually, Blaine muttered an oath. "Christ's teeth, they really hate him."

Tavish's mouth thinned, although his gaze remained riveted upon the gateway. "Aye," he murmured. "Fear isn't the same thing as respect ... something Roy and our father never learned."

Seated by the fire in the solar, Robina finished a neat stitch and held up the pillowcase to admire. It was a cluster of yellow daisies—a design that made her yearn for the warmth of summer.

Heaving a sigh, she lowered her embroidery to her lap and shifted her attention to the dancing flames in the hearth.

She'd taken her noon meal alone up here and had been grateful for the solitude. After the violence and fury of the morning, she needed to be on her own for a while.

It was warm and peaceful in the solar, and sleepiness descended upon her.

Perhaps it was a reaction to shock, but she felt as if she could fall asleep in her chair.

However, the solar door whooshed open then, and a tall dark figure entered, intruding upon her solitude.

Tavish closed the door behind him, his lean face tense as his attention swept to her.

The impact of their gazes meeting made a frisson of heat ignite in the pit of Robina's belly, her sleepiness dissipating.

When Tavish spoke, his voice was both rough and soft, tension emanating off him. "Robina, we need to talk."

17

OUR SECRET

"AYE," ROBINA MURMURED, casting aside her embroidery. "We do."

Tavish crossed the solar and halted before her. Robina didn't want to remain seated, to crane her neck up to hold his gaze, and so she rose to her feet.

"Firstly, I must give ye my thanks," he said, his throat bobbing. "Yer help this morning was appreciated."

Robina huffed a nervous laugh. The intensity of his stare was putting her on edge, as was his strange formality. "Ye would have likely overpowered Roy on yer own ... but I had to do something."

"Ye did well." He stepped closer to her, his gaze roaming her face. "The bastard would have knifed me in the back if ye hadn't warned me."

Robina swallowed. There was no arguing that. "Are ye sorry he's gone?" she asked after a pause. "I know Roy tried to kill ye ... but he's kin after all."

Tavish's face tensed, and a shadow moved in the depths of his eyes. "Part of me is sorry, aye," he said, his voice developing a husky edge. "But, after what he did, Roy had to go."

Robina nodded. She understood. Attempted murder wasn't something Tavish could overlook, and it was a relief to know that Roy's presence, and his aggression, had been removed from Castle Gunn.

Tavish held her gaze, silence stretching between them for a few moments before he cleared his throat. "Secondly, I must ask yer forgiveness," he continued. "I've acted like an arse, Robina."

She inclined her head, surprise feathering within her. However, she didn't speak—instead letting him elaborate.

"Fear made a coward of me," he said softly, reaching out and taking her hands. "For years, I've dreamed of having ye as my wife, but when that day came ... and ye gave me what I wished for ... the reality of what that actually meant suddenly terrified me." His face twisted then, and she knew these words were costing her proud husband. Yet she remained silent, allowing him to explain himself further.

"I don't know how to give of myself," he said finally. "I've never let anyone in before."

Robina gently squeezed his hands. "Neither have I," she whispered. "I arrived here determined to hate ye, Tavish Gunn ... and I almost succeeded ... yet ye won me over."

His grey eyes shadowed. "And then I hurt ye ... I'm sorry, mo chridhe."

Robina's throat thickened. "I'm scared too," she said, her voice husky now. "I'm not used to being seen ... I too worry that if I trust too deeply, I'll have my heart ripped out."

His grip on her hands grew firmer then before he lifted one of her hands to his lips and bestowed a kiss upon the back of it. "Yer heart will always be safe with me, my love. I made ye a pledge, and I intend to honor it. I promise to cherish ye as ye so deserve."

Robina's vision misted, the pressure in her throat increasing. "I love ye, Tavish," she whispered, "and when I thought Roy was going to kill ye, it was as if the world stopped."

His mouth came down upon hers then, fierce, desperate, and he hauled her into his arms.

Robina kissed him back with the same desperation, her lips parting eagerly under his. The strength of his arms about her, the taste and scent of him, filled her senses.

She craved him like sunlight after a bitter winter.

His mouth never leaving hers, Tavish swiveled around and walked her back so that her backside hit the edge of the table that dominated the solar. And then he lifted her up onto it.

Robina reached up, her fingers tangling in his silky, unbound hair as their kisses grew deeper, hungrier—a clash of teeth and a tangle of tongues.

He reached down, fisting her skirts and drawing them up, his fingers sliding over the skin beneath.

Robina eagerly parted her thighs for him, gasping as he slid a finger deep into her. She was already so wet for him, so needy.

Her hands trailed down over his gambeson to the waistband of his braies, and she released him. Her fingertips traced the iron-hard, velvety length of his shaft, marveling at its beauty, at how it leaked at the crown.

He too yearned for their joining.

"Do ye see what ye do to me, mo ghràdh?" he growled.

My love.

He slid a second finger into her then, and a groan tore from Robina's throat. "Aye," she gasped. "Oh, aye … Tavish!"

The way he was touching her, the slick glide of his fingers, made her quiver around him.

With a muttered oath, he removed his questing fingers, spread her wide, and drove his shaft into her in one deep thrust.

Robina's throaty cry echoed around the solar. She wrapped her legs around his hips and lifted her hips, bringing him deeper still, as he thrust into her once more.

And all the while, their gazes remained fused—the intimacy of it rending.

It was almost too much, to hold her husband's gaze as he rode her. The raw look on his face, the fierceness in his eyes, made wildness quicken within her.

And then something deep inside unraveled, and Robina shattered around him. Her body quivered, her head falling back as pleasure crested and carried her off.

"Robina!" Tavish's raw cry joined her own. "My love, my heart!"

He thrust into her fiercely then, his fingers digging into her hips. She glanced up to see that he was struggling to keep control. "I can't," he grunted. "I want to ... but—"

"Let go, my love," she gasped, undulating her hips in a sensual roll that made her breathing catch. "Fall into me."

The look on his face then, the naked vulnerability of it, made tears blur her vision. She rolled her hips once more, tightening her core around him as she dug her heels into his buttocks, drawing him deeper still.

Tavish's raw cry shook the solar, and she watched transfixed, as he reared above her, his face twisting as if he were in agony. An instant later, he stiffened, and she felt the hot rush of his release inside her.

Panting, he reached for Robina, pulling her up so that he could hold her.

Likewise, Robina wound her arms about his torso, holding on tight as if they were being buffeted by a violent storm.

She could feel the tremble in his body, the tension in the lean muscles of his back—and when she raised a hand to his cheek, she realized it was wet with tears.

Tavish clung to his wife in the aftermath of their coupling. He had to hold her tight, for if he let her go, he would crumble to dust.

Robina dredged up emotions within him that he didn't even realize he possessed, emotions that brought up memories long buried: the grief and loneliness of losing his mother, the sickening fear as he'd watched his father beat his elder brother, Alex, half to death years earlier.

His wife tore down his defenses; she made everything rush in.

And as he held her tight, aware that hot tears now slicked his cheeks, he realized he'd never felt so scared, exposed—or alive.

Gradually, the rawness of the moment drew back, and Tavish lifted a shaky hand, tangling it in his wife's soft tresses. And when he leaned back, his gaze finding hers once more, he saw that her hazel eyes gleamed with love.

"Ye aren't to tell anyone about my soft underbelly," he murmured, as she reached out and brushed away the last of his tears. "If my brothers ever discovered that my wife made me weep like a maid, I'd never hear the end of it."

Robina's throaty laugh surprised him. Her soft pink mouth curved into an impish smile. "It will be our secret," she replied huskily. She then slid closer to him, wrapping her legs even more firmly around his hips.

Still buried deep inside her, Tavish felt his rod stiffen. Her gaze widened then, her smile softening into a deeply sensual expression.

"Why don't ye carry me to bed," she murmured, "and reveal some more secrets?" The husky rasp to her voice inflamed him further still, and when she squirmed against him, Tavish's breathing caught.

"Aye, wife," he growled, sliding his hands under her naked bottom and lifting her off the table. "And let us see if I can make ye do the same."

And with that, he carried her into the bed-chamber.

EPILOGUE

THE GIFT

Three months later ...

A SMILE CURVED Robina's lips as she watched Thistle glide high above the castle. An instant later, the goshawk spied prey on the ground and dove.

Robina's breathing caught as the bird plummeted—swift, silent, and deadly—and plucked something small off the lush green meadow to the north of the castle.

Around her, the signs of spring were everywhere: bulbs poking up from the damp earth and newborn lambs and goat kids frolicking around on the hills west of the castle.

It was a blustery morning. The sea to the east was a mass of foaming whitecaps, yet the wind was from the south and carried with it the scent of grass and blossom.

Robina's smile widened. Winter, and all the upheaval it had brought into their lives, was behind them.

Once Thistle had gobbled down the hapless creature—most likely a field mouse—she flew back to Robina, landing upon her glove.

"Well done, my lovely," Robina murmured as she made her way back to the mews. "Ye will have to boast to yer sister of yer deed."

Thistle favored her with an arch look, as if such things were beneath her, but Robina paid her no mind.

She was used to her goshawks' imperious looks—it was one of the things she loved about them.

Inside the mews, she interrupted Malcolm stealing a kiss from Fiona. The maid had ventured upstairs with Robina before ducking in to see him.

Breaking apart, they both cast her an embarrassed look, and Fiona's cheeks went a charming shade of pink. Judging by the lustiness of their embrace, Robina wondered if Castle Gunn would see another wedding by mid-summer.

"Don't mind me," she said cheerfully, placing Thistle back on her perch next to her sister and fastening her leash.

Malcolm ducked his head. "Did yer goshawk have a successful hunt, Lady Robina?"

"Aye ... a field mouse caught her eye, I believe," Robina replied. She noted the way Malcolm and Fiona eyed each other. The atmosphere inside the mews was charged, as if they couldn't wait to resume the kiss she'd interrupted. "I will take Moth out after the noon meal."

She left the mews moments later, shutting the door behind her with a smile, and made her way downstairs. There was something about seeing two people so obviously smitten with each other that warmed her soul.

For years, she'd only had her parents' union as a model—and her mother and nurse's bitter, poisonous words to form a distorted picture of relations between husband and wife.

Robina's smile widened. She now knew better.

She found her husband outside the stables, shoeing his courser. Old Misty sat a few yards from her master, although the Highland Collie rose to her feet and went to greet Robina as she approached.

Lowering one of the hind hooves he'd just shod, Tavish flashed Robina a smile.

And as always, the sight of him made Robina's belly flutter. Three moons had passed since Roy had been driven from the castle and the last reserves had dropped between them, and the time since had been a joyful discovery.

Robina liked that she and Tavish were inseparable these days. They often hawked and hunted together, and her brothers-by-marriage had gotten used to her accompanying them on stag and boar hunts. Robina might have been slender and slight of build, but she had a stout heart and a sense of adventure they'd all come to appreciate.

Will, who was rubbing his horse down a few yards away, waved to her, and Robina favored him with a smile in return.

Ever since Roy's departure, a shadow had lifted from Castle Gunn. Relations between the remaining brothers had improved, and the rivalry that had once characterized their rapport had eased a little.

Tavish had relaxed into the role of clan-chief, and it pleased Robina that he now smiled often.

"How are Moth and Thistle?" he asked with a grin.

"Enjoying the sunshine," she replied, "as am I."

"Do ye want to go for a ride before the noon meal?" he asked, slapping his stallion's rump. "Thorn is almost shod ... and itching to stretch his legs."

Robina nodded, her heart lightening farther at the suggestion. Her husband knew she loved to get out of the castle regularly. "Aye, I shall go and ready one of the garrons."

"Wait," Tavish replied, still grinning. "There's someone I'd like ye to meet first." He stepped forward then, taking her hand and leading her into the stables.

Intrigued, Robina cut him a questioning look, yet her husband merely winked and led her to the furthest stall from the door.

And there she found a beautiful, leggy chestnut mare.

The horse greeted Tavish with a whicker, nudging at him, before she swung her head over to Robina and snorted softly.

"Hello, lass," Robina breathed, stroking the courser's face. She then shot her husband a look, smiling widely. "Is she mine?"

"Aye ... if ye wish to keep her?"

"Of course I do, she's lovely." Robina couldn't stop smiling as she let the mare snuffle at her neck. "What's her name?"

"Amber ... but ye can change it if ye wish."

"No, Amber is a fine name." Robina squeezed his hand she still held. "When did ye sneak her in here?"

"Yesterday afternoon ... I bought her at the Lybster horse market. On a whim." He paused then. "I thought it time ye ride something other than a pony."

Robina's throat constricted as their gazes met. "She is a bonny gift, Tav ... the best ... like ye." She leaned into him then, and they shared a lingering, tender kiss.

When she drew back, Robina's chest ached with tenderness and she noted that her husband's grey eyes gleamed.

"I'm glad ye are pleased," he said gruffly. "I thought it was time I spoiled ye."

A smile flowered across Robina's face. "Ye spoil me daily, husband ... I risk becoming a thoroughly pampered lady."

"And ye are worth every bit of it," he said huskily, reaching up and stroking her cheek. "Plus, ye make me feel like the luckiest man alive ... I wanted to do this for ye." Next to them, Amber snorted, irritated at being ignored.

A moment later, something nudged Robina's leg. She glanced down to see that Misty had followed her into the stables. The collie was gazing up at her with soft brown eyes, making it clear that she, too, was feeling neglected.

Smiling, Robina reached down and stroked the dog's head. She then met her husband's eye once more. "Thank ye, Tav," she murmured. Her smile widened, excitement fluttering within her. "I'll saddle her now, and we can race."

He favored her with a masculine, indulgent grin in return. "Amber won't outrun Thorn, my love."

Robina lifted her chin, her look issuing him a direct challenge. Aye, he rode a powerful stallion, yet he clearly hadn't noticed Amber's long, finely-boned legs. Anyone could see the mare was swift. "We shall see about that," she replied.

The End

FROM THE AUTHOR

I hope you enjoyed Robina and Tavish's emotional, and steamy, story! I introduced these two during HIGHLANDER FORBIDDEN and just couldn't forget about them. And as soon as I started work on this tale, I was hooked. I'm a bit of a sucker for arranged marriage stories, and of course, Historical Romance gives me the perfect opportunity to write them.

I adore both characters, their blend of strength and vulnerability, and how they are each other's safe haven. I also enjoyed setting it around Christmas—my favorite time of year!

This story takes place at Castle Gunn, a real location. The fortress, also known as Gunn's Castle and Clyth Castle, is situated on a rock above the sea, eight miles southwest of Wick, Caithness. It was once a splendid and strong castle. Sadly, virtually nothing remains of it these days.

Jayne x

ABOUT THE AUTHOR

Award-winning author Jayne Castel writes epic Historical and Fantasy Romance. Her vibrant characters, richly researched historical settings, and action-packed adventure romance transport readers to forgotten times and imaginary worlds.

Jayne has published a number of bestselling series. In love with all things Scottish, Jayne also writes romances set in Dark Ages Scotland ... sexy Pict warriors anyone?

When she's not writing, Jayne is reading (and re-reading) her favorite authors, cooking Italian feasts, and going for long walks with her husband. She lives in New Zealand's beautiful South Island.

Connect with Jayne online:
www.jaynecastel.com
www.facebook.com/JayneCastelRomance/
https://www.instagram.com/jaynecastelauthor/
Email: contact@jaynecastel.com

Printed in Great Britain
by Amazon